HUNTRESS

by Renee Carter Hall

Huntress

Copyright © 2015 by Renee Carter Hall

Cover illustration by Sekhmet

Published by FurPlanet Productions
Dallas, TX
http://www.FurPlanet.com

ISBN 978-1-61450-279-1

Printed in the United States of America
First Edition Trade Paperback 2015

"Huntress" © 2013 Renee Carter Hall; first appeared in the anthology *Five Fortunes*, published by FurPlanet Productions. "The Shape of the Sky," "Kamara and the Star-Beast," and "Where the Rivers Meet" © 2015 Renee Carter Hall; original to this edition.

*For my grandmothers,
my mother,
and my sister,
who taught me the many ways
that women can be strong.*

TABLE OF CONTENTS

HUNTRESS

CHAPTER 1

Leya gripped the spear tighter and edged forward another step, careful not to rise out of her crouch, staying as low as she could. A breeze swayed the tall grasses before her, but the lioness' pale gold coat kept her hidden. She wore only a hide loincloth, and she'd even cut the beads off of it so she could move more quietly. Her prey was in sight now, locked in her gaze. It was cropping grass calmly just a few lengths ahead, facing away from her, unaware of the mortal danger it was in…

"Um, Leya?" Bahati's voice drifted back to her. "The wind's blowing this way. I can smell you. Should I run?"

Leya swore under her breath, stood up, and flung the spear as hard as she could, not bothering to see where it landed. It wasn't a real weapon anyway, just a straight stick smoothed to a rounded point, the right length and weight for practice.

A pretend spear for a pretend huntress, she thought, disgusted at herself for forgetting something as simple as the wind.

Bahati, her "prey," stood up, brushed dust and bits of grass from his fur and loincloth, and searched through the long grass to bring the spear back to her. "Easy on that; it's the last one we've got. And I'm not making you any more if you're just going to keep breaking them, you know."

He said it teasingly, but Leya stalked off. "Some *karanja*

I'll make," she muttered. "I'd never even get close."

Bahati followed her as she picked up the trail leading back to Lwazi, their village. "It'll get easier. Remember the stories? Even Kamara couldn't catch anything at first."

"Only because of the moonlight," Leya retorted, "before she prayed to Yaa to cover the moon with his mane."

"Oh. Yeah, I... forgot about that part."

Leya shook her head. She knew the stories well enough. Kamara the Huntress had killed a zebra foal when she was a flat-chested cub. No *karanja* would ever expect any mortal to be that good, but she'd still have to prove herself worthy of training.

Bahati walked beside her in silence. He had been her best friend almost as long as she could remember, but there were some things she knew she couldn't expect him to understand. Nothing ever worried him for long; he was steady as sunrise, always ready with a smile or a joke, and moved through life as if it were nothing more than a game or a dance. The simplest things pleased him: a beautiful sunset, fresh honeycomb, watching a line of ants. He didn't seem to have much ambition himself, though he was training now for a place in the *aumah's* guard, as all the young males did if they chose not to leave the village after ascension. He seemed to live looking no farther ahead than the next morning, but for Leya, each day was merely another mark of time before her real life would begin, far from the village, among the red ochre tents of the *karanja*.

The first time she'd seen them, she had been very young, but she hadn't been afraid. The other cubs, male and female alike, had hidden behind their mothers, frightened by the huntresses' fierce eyes and sharp weapons. Where the villagers wore beads or stones, the *karanja* sported necklaces of bone and hoof and claw, and their loincloths were made of zebra hide in deference to Kamara's first kill, a material only they were permitted to wear.

They were all mesmerizing, exotic and dangerous and beautiful, their eyeshine flashing like lightning-strikes as they took their places around the fire. But there was one Leya could not look away from.

Masika, the *karanjala*, first among the *karanja*. Her headdress of fish-eagle feathers stood out from her noble face like a mane, and her loincloth was of giraffe hide, just as their first male wore. Her eyes were sharp and watchful, her every muscle toned and tensed, and like all the *karanja*, she proudly bore the twin scars on her chest where her breasts had been cut away. Leya sat silently, drinking in Masika's presence, watching everything the huntress did, every movement, every manner.

A cricket landed within the circle, almost at Masika's feet, very near the fire.

Leya leapt without thinking, throwing the whole force of her small body toward her prey. The cricket arced away neatly, and Leya's finger-pads touched the red-hot embers.

Leya jerked away with a cry of pain and surprise, tears welling in her eyes. Her mother was already rushing to her, but it was Masika who picked her up and held her in that beautiful, terrible gaze.

The huntress smiled. "Take heart, little one. It may live today, but you live as well, and you will be stronger when you meet it next."

Leya forgot the pain in her fingers, forgot everything but that gaze, that smile, those words that lit the heat of hope in her chest. She blinked back her tears and tried to smile back.

"This one has the heart of the *karanja*," Masika said. "She would follow her prey into the fire itself."

Masika turned and handed Leya to her mother. "She has fierce eyes for one so young. Keep her close, or she may follow our path."

Leya looked to her mother. She thought her mother would be happy to hear such praise, but instead Naimah's ears went back and she looked at the ground when she spoke. "If she so chooses."

Now, of course, Leya understood. The *karanja* lived apart, did not take mates, did not bear cubs. They were meant for something more, something greater.

And so was she.

◙ ⚙ ◙

Leya left the spear at the back of the hut, away from the stack of firewood but where she hoped her mother wouldn't see it. Naimah was out front at the grinding-stone, turning handfuls of millet into coarse flour. She didn't look up when Leya approached, instead keeping her attention on the long stone she was rolling back and forth in a steady rhythm.

"Where have you been?" Naimah asked.

"Out. With Bahati." She knew her mother wouldn't question that any further, would fill in the spaces with her own hopes.

Ever since Leya had reached adulthood at the last rains, her mother had been pestering her about Bahati. He was handsome. He was strong. He was kind. His cubs would be strong, and he would be a good father. The village rainspeaker—who knew many things of this world and the next—had said once that Bahati was the second birth of the spirit of an ancient *aumah*, a ruler of their people. He might even be an *aumah* himself one day, who knew? Her mother sent these compliments out like a swarm of black flies, buzzing around Leya constantly.

"I don't want to be an *aumah*'s wife," Leya had said one day. Underneath that were the words she didn't say, the words her mother still heard. *I don't want to be anyone's wife.*

The worst of it was, sometimes those black flies still buzzed around when she was with Bahati. And she could see all of it. He was handsome, of course, with his golden mane almost full now, his body lean and strong. Anyone could see that. Even the white-muzzled lionesses, sway-breasted and half-blind, murmured among themselves when Bahati walked by. And he was patient. He carved whistles and roarers and spears for the boy-cubs, when most males his age paid no attention to anyone younger. He even carried water for old Sisi, who spent all day lying on her mat in her hut and was too old and tired to walk to the river anymore. Of course Leya liked him; *everyone* liked him.

But she could not be his mate.

Naimah swept the flour into a basket, added another handful of grain to the flat stone, and started the rhythm again. "Ayanna was asking for you."

Leya felt a thorn-prick of guilt. "Why?"

"They're making her necklaces today. Did you forget?"

Leya swallowed the curse just in time. "Are they done?"

"Not for a long while yet. They're slow, those girls. More talking than working." Naimah paused, then smiled slightly, her eyes distant. "But I remember how it was." She glanced back at Leya. "Go on. Better not make them angry with you, or there'll be no one to make yours later."

Leya ignored that and set off at a trot to the fire-circle in the center of the village. The others were already there, a half-dozen girl-cubs born in Ayanna's and Leya's season. Ayanna sat in the middle of them, as if she were going to be the *aumah*'s wife herself, instead of marrying a male with a half-grown mane, someone Leya had never seen anything special about. But Ayanna had talked of nothing and no one else since the two of them had started walking together, so Leya figured there had to be something about him worth loving, even if she couldn't see it. Even now, there was a light in the young lioness' eyes that Leya didn't entirely understand but somehow still envied. It wasn't just being happy; it was being satisfied and content and excited all at once. She was glad for Ayanna, even though they'd never been that close.

It was custom for the other females Ayanna's age to string beads for her bridal necklaces. The more she wore that day, the longer and happier her life with her husband would be. There were beads of clay and stone and wood and ostrich eggshell, all neatly grouped in bowls, and Leya grabbed the closest bowl and a thorn needle and started in, trying to work quickly to make up for being late.

One of the lionesses giggled suddenly, and then others joined in. Leya glanced up, not sure of the joke, looking from one to the next for clues.

Even Ayanna was trying not to laugh, looking at Leya's strand of beads. "Jasiri's blood is hot enough, I know," she said, "but I'm not sure I'd want *that* many."

Leya looked down at the beads, trying to piece things together, and then remembered that each one had a meaning. The ones she'd used represented how many cubs a wife would bear, and were meant to be scattered through a pattern of other beads. The way she'd strung so many one after the other, Ayanna would be bearing cubs three at a time for the rest of her life.

Leya's ears burned as she tried to think of something to say, to be in on the joke instead of the one they were laughing at. "Well, I've seen how he looks at you. You'll be carrying by the time the rains come again."

Ayanna's ears flushed, too, with a mixture of pride and modesty. One of the others dropped her voice to a whisper and told a joke she'd heard from an aunt, about a young groom who didn't want to wait for his wedding, and a trick his bride played on him.

Leya laughed with the others, though she found the joke

silly. When they were younger, she'd spent most of her time playing with the boy-cubs, pretending to be heroes and enemies, seeing who could throw a melon the farthest before they'd all gotten caught and whipped for wasting food. Now, ever since her body had changed and made her a woman— and a potential wife—she was thrown back into the other females' company, to find them speaking a language she'd never learned.

She started a new string of beads, slipped and jabbed a finger-pad with her needle, then quietly set aside three beads she'd bled on. She didn't know what that would symbolize in a bridal necklace, but it probably wouldn't be good. As they worked, the others chattered and whooped like baboons, telling jokes, sharing stories of when they'd all been cubs together. Leya was never mentioned, of course; she hadn't been there most of the time, or at least not with them. When they'd played a prank once using a basket of ants, Leya and two of the boys had been the ones gathering the ants. She thought about telling them how many times she'd been bitten that day, and how one of the boys had cried from the pain, but instead she kept silent, stringing beads the way her mother ground the flour, a slow and steady rhythm, letting the conversation buzz around her, all the time feeling like an elephant in a herd of gazelle.

By the time they were done, it was almost sunset. Each lioness slipped her finished necklace over Ayanna's head and embraced her. Leya came last, hesitating with her mismatched strand, deciding what to say. Ayanna looked strangely grown up suddenly, like a stranger from some other village, beautiful in her honey-colored coat and layers of bright necklaces. She looked like she already knew the answers to questions Leya hadn't even thought of yet.

Leya swallowed. "I don't know anything about… any of this. But I hope you'll be happy. As happy as you are now, always." She started to put the necklace on Ayanna, then stopped. The others looked so perfect, and somehow hers didn't match any of them, even though they'd all used the same beads.

Ayanna smiled, took Leya's wrists gently, and slipped the necklace over her head with the others. "I'm glad you came."

Afterward, restless and craving solitude, Leya went out to check her snares. She had three, set just beyond the boundaries of the village. It was, to her mind, a lesser way to hunt, but then she was limited to lesser prey anyway. Only *karanja* and a village's *aumah* could kill the heavy meat. Everyone else could take only light meat—birds or fish, scrub hare, or at most, the red pigs that sometimes rooted through the village crops. She'd hoped to kill one of the pigs before the *karanja* arrived again, but so far they'd been too fast and too smart for her, especially since her only real weapon was the short ivory-handled knife her mother had given her when she'd become an adult. All women carried them, for foraging or preparing food, but Leya had secretly honed her blade until it was sharp enough to shave fur from her skin.

It was already dark by the time she reached the last snare and found a grouse hen floundering, flapping its wings uselessly. She snapped its neck, enjoying the feel of its limp weight as she followed the trail back toward the village. One day, she would come back to the clan with the other *karanja*, after a great hunt, bearing a full zebra, the hide still on—

No. Too common.

A young elephant, then, a suckling calf, the meat tender and nut-sweet, with its rich shining liver to present to the *aumah*. They would come carrying it to the fireside, singing one of their chants, the villagers clapping and keeping time, cubs dancing in the ruddy light, and all would eat until they could eat no more. She smiled, picturing it.

But, as her mother was fond of saying, dreams tasted

good on the tongue but left your belly empty. She had to become a *karanja* first.

The glow of a small fire and a low, pulsing rhythm in the distance caught her attention. She'd forgotten they were drumming tonight, as part of the bridal celebration that would stretch for days.

Leya crept closer, keeping back to the shadows, low in the grass, checking the wind this time to make sure it didn't carry her scent. Only the males were allowed at these private circles, but even when she'd been little she'd loved to sneak away to watch.

Bahati was among them, playing the twin drums he'd made himself, adding counterpoints to the larger instruments, weaving in and out of their rhythm, circling it, deepening it. He barely looked as if he were concentrating at all.

Of course the males competed among themselves, but this was not the fierce, solemn challenge of the duels, or even the proud sport of the annual games. This was a friendly match of grins and taunts, each trying to best the others, showing off among those who could truly appreciate the skill.

Leya watched, forgetting everything else. Bahati's hands blurred across the drums. His eyes flashed with triumph—and joy, she realized, pure joy like a cub at play.

She envied him. He could do this, could be alive in this moment, could do something he was obviously born to do, and yet it didn't consume him the way her desires did. Tonight after the fire had died down to embers, he would go back to his hut, place the drums back in their spot by his mat, and sleep. He wouldn't lie awake thinking of what he could have done differently, could have done better. He wouldn't stare into the darkness, afraid of never being what he wished to be, never being good enough to earn the respect he longed for.

The hen she carried had gone stiff. She allowed herself one last glance at the circle, then moved on until the drumming faded into the sounds of the night.

回 ✿ 回

The next morning, when she checked the snares again, she saw the red tents on the horizon. They were barely specks, and she had to squint to make sure they were really there and not just a trick of the mist that hung in layers over the savannah.

She stared at the tents as if she could will them closer. They were still a few days away, from the look of it, even at the pace they kept.

Bahati caught up with her on her way back to the trail. "Anything in the snares?"

She shook her head. "Empty. But I had a grouse last night."

As they walked, she thought back to the drumming circle, how she had watched him. She almost wanted to tell him she'd been there—he would never tell anyone else—but something about it made her feel shy in a way she'd never felt around him before.

His voice broke in on her thoughts. "Have you talked to your mother yet?"

"Not yet."

"Have you… thought about talking to her?"

Leya sighed. "I was hoping I wouldn't have to." Even as she said it, she knew how stupid it sounded, as if she were simply going to leave with the *karanja* and maybe Masika would tell Leya's mother she was going. *You want to run down zebra and kudu and wildebeest,* she scolded herself, *and you're afraid to face your own mother.*

"She can't stop you," Bahati said, as if hearing Leya's thoughts. "No one can."

"I know. It's just that I've tried to tell her before, and she only hears what she wants to hear. She thinks I'm going to change my mind, that I'm going to fall in love and spend the rest of my life raising cubs like everybody else, and then she'll be happy."

"There's nothing wrong with love. I hear it's… kind of nice, actually."

"No, but she acts like it's everything. They all act like it's everything. Like there's nothing else I could want to do." She thought again of Ayanna, that light in her eyes. She tried to imagine wearing those bridal necklaces herself, how it might feel to have their weight resting at her breastbone.

She stopped and looked back at Bahati. "What do you mean, you hear it's kind of nice?"

For possibly the first time since she'd known him, Bahati looked embarrassed. It made him look like a cub again, and she pounced on the expression. "You wouldn't know anything about it yourself, would you?"

He looked away. "Maybe."

"Who?"

He kept his eyes on the trail ahead and didn't answer.

"Come on, Bahati. You know I can't guess—you could have any woman in the village. It's always Bahati this and Bahati that, kind and strong and gentle and handsome…" She trailed off into a laugh, enjoying the red flush of his ears half-hidden by his golden mane. "Whoever it is, I won't tell her. I promise. You know I don't talk to any of them anyway."

Bahati shook his head. "Never mind. It's not important."

"Does she know?"

He didn't look at her. "No. She doesn't."

"Are you going to tell her?"

He looked at the ground. "I don't know. Maybe. Maybe not."

They had reached the village. Leya faced him, crossing his arms. "We'll make a deal, then. I'll tell my mother tonight about wanting to join the *karanja*. And you'll tell your future wife how beautiful you think she is, or whatever else you're supposed to say. Deal?" She held out her right hand, palm up, to show she had nothing to hide.

Bahati paused. "All right," he said softly, and brushed her palm with his.

回{۞}回

Leya found her mother already in the middle of cooking three different things. Every time the red tents were spotted, the village became busier than a termite mound, ready to welcome the huntresses and give gifts to thank them for the fresh and smoked meat they brought. Naimah, though, always worked harder than any of the other women, roasting grain, pounding yams, brewing honey-beer for the celebration, baking stack after stack of dry flatbread for the *karanja* to take with them. She had never seemed to like the *karanja* and indeed seemed to avoid them as much as she could, but somehow whenever they arrived, she worried that things wouldn't be right, that the food might be burned or dry or spoiled, or that there wouldn't be enough, as if she cared very much what they thought.

Leya brought more water and firewood without being asked. Then she sat just inside the hut, far enough from her mother to be out of the way but close enough to be easily heard. "Mother..."

"Mm?"

"I've been meaning to tell you something."

Her mother put down the pounding-stick she'd been using on the yams and turned to face her. Naimah's expression was neither excited nor surprised, but there was a flicker of something in her eyes that gave Leya courage to go on.

"It's about the *karanja*."

The flicker died like an oil lamp blown out. Leya swallowed. "I'm going to take the initiation when they come."

Naimah went back to pounding yams as if the future of the village depended on them being mashed to precisely the right smoothness. "You're too young. Wait another year; things might be different."

"I'm not waiting another year, Mother. *This* year. Now. I just... wanted you to know. Before they came."

Naimah shook her head slowly. Silence grew between them, bloated between them like something dead. Leya started to think about bringing in more firewood.

"That's not the life I want for you," her mother said softly.

"It's what I want for myself." She meant it to come out strong and sharp, but instead it was barely a whisper.

Naimah put aside the pounding-stick and began stirring the mashed yams. "When you were born, the rainspeaker said your soul was like a bird caught in a net, and would always be struggling to get free. I didn't know what he meant. I still don't know." She sighed. "You know they don't take everyone."

"I know." Over the years, she'd asked everyone she could about the initiation, even old Sisi before she'd started to forget things. No one could tell her what it was; apparently Masika would take her off into the veld by herself, and whatever would happen, would happen there, out of sight of everyone, and she would be forbidden to talk about it. There were plenty of rumors about what the *karanjala* might demand of an initiate, everything from seeing how far she could throw a spear to how long she could go without food, and she'd heard one whispered story involving ants and smears of honey in particular places. She'd done her best to practice as much as she could, though she'd left the ants alone, hoping that was just the sort of story girl-cubs told to frighten each other.

"Well." Naimah took up handfuls of the mashed yams

and began shaping them into flattened rounds. "I can't hold you here. You know that."

"I know," Leya said again. But she didn't want to just be let go. She wanted to be sent off, with hope and good wishes, like Ayanna was being sent into marriage with ropes of beads for good luck, every strand made from friendship and love.

Still… Maybe being let go was enough. It was at least better than leaving in defiance or slipping away without a word.

Naimah plucked a piece of flatbread from one of the stacks and handed it to Leya. "Here. You'd better get used to eating this." Then she picked up the calabash they used for carrying water, balanced it on her head with an ease Leya still marveled at, and set off for the trail to the river.

Leya took a bite of the bread. It tasted like nothing, like grit, like the taste of her own mouth. She made herself finish it anyway, though she shuddered when the last bite went down.

◧ ❀ ◩

The next morning, the tents were a little closer, and Leya thought she could even see figures moving around them as each one disappeared, though the morning mist made it hard to be sure. Once the tents had all been packed up, she stretched out on the warm rock, gazing up into the cloudless blue sky. When she was little, she'd thought of the sky as a lake, and dreamed of dipping a calabash into it and seeing what it tasted like. She'd always thought it would be sweeter somehow than regular water, more like honey or juice, and it would make her strong, and she'd be able to do anything she wanted.

Well, at least now her mother knew. If she passed the initiation, she would leave with the *karanja*. So that was all right. She closed her eyes, letting the feeling sink in. It would be a long journey, but at last she was on her way.

Something dropped onto her belly.

Leya opened her eyes. A tiny rock lizard stared back at her, its blue head cocked. She sighed, herded the lizard off her and onto the rock, and looked up. "Bahati."

"That's all I get? I knew I should have saved it for Milele. *She* would have screamed."

Leya sat up, and Bahati sat next to her, drawing his knees up to his chest. "Is Milele who you talked to last night?" she asked. "She's pretty enough, but I thought you'd want someone smarter."

"No, I did not talk to Milele last night."

"So who was it?"

He shook his head. "You first. How did it go?"

"All right, I guess." She shrugged. "She didn't cry or yell or anything."

"She'll be better when she sees you're happy. She's just afraid right now you won't be."

"Yes, *aumah*." She watched the rock lizard skitter into a crevice and disappear. "So…?"

"I didn't talk to her."

"That's the last time I make a bargain with you, then."

"It doesn't matter, anyway."

"Of course it matters. Don't you want a wife?"

"I do." He traced a rough edge of stone with his fingertips. "Very much. But she doesn't want me."

"How do you know?"

She'd never heard Bahati's voice so muted and soft. "I just do. It's not in her eyes when she looks at me. The way I know it's in mine."

"She's an idiot, then. Any woman in the village would want you." Leya stared back up at the sky. "It's better I don't know who she is. I'd just tell her how stupid I think she is."

Bahati chuckled. "I don't think it would do any good."

He stretched out next to her, and she moved closer, closing her eyes again, breathing in the scent of warm stone and the faint musk of Bahati's fur. She was lucky to have him for a friend, she knew, lucky to have had him all these years to talk to. She felt safe around him—not safe from danger, exactly, but comfortable in a way she couldn't be with anyone else. She would miss that, when she was gone.

回 ۞ 回

The next morning, the red tents were unmistakable on the horizon. Ayanna went into her mother's hut, not to be seen again until the wedding. Leya ate another piece of flatbread and told herself she was getting used to the taste, or the lack of it. She tried to find Bahati, to practice with him one more time before the *karanja* arrived, but he wasn't in the village. She checked their favorite spots without any sign of him, then shrugged and went to her snares.

The first one was empty, though it looked like something had been caught in it and torn free. She tied a new knot in the noose, replaced the trigger sticks, and went on to the second one.

Before she got close, she knew she had something, though she wasn't sure what. It was something small and light-colored, making a faint strangled noise that was almost a bleat. She broke into a trot.

It was a gazelle, one of the little ones, a newborn out of season, lying almost on its back with one hind leg waving. The herds didn't normally travel this close to the village, but maybe having the *karanja* nearby had spooked a small group into new territory.

She watched it for a few minutes, wondering how long it had been struggling there. It barely moved now except for fast, shallow breaths.

Heavy meat. She couldn't kill it. She cut the snare from its neck, sat back on her haunches, and waited for the fawn to get up, but either something had broken or the fawn had no strength left to stand and run. Instead it lay there, eyes dull, one leg jerking aimlessly now and then.

Leya stood. She knew she should walk away, check the next snare for something she could use. This prey was the veld's, not hers. If she were *karanja*, she could cut its throat, slice its belly, take it into her, use its strength.

She was not *karanja*, not yet.

They ate their meat raw, she had heard, though she'd only ever seen them eat it cooked in the village. It was said the blood made them strong, gave them courage.

She needed strength. She needed courage.

Leya's hand went to her knife. It was sharp enough. She checked the wind, listened carefully, scanned the grasses around her. She was alone. No one would see.

The fawn watched her. It had stopped moving but still breathed.

She could let it die and then eat it right away. It would not be right, but it would be more right than killing it herself.

She imagined it larger, imagined a spear instead of a knife. She had never done anything but snap the necks of grouse or scrub hare. When that moment came on the veld, she could not hesitate, or it might mean her own life. This, then, was practice.

She carried the fawn farther into the grasses, away from where the snare had been. When she thought she was far enough away, she went a little farther. At last she crouched, pulled the fawn's head up with one hand, gripped her knife in the other, and cut deep.

When the first spray of blood had slowed, she slit its belly. It was not so different from a scrub hare, she decided, once it was opened, and that comforted her a little. She waved away the flies and went on, cutting a chunk from the fawn's flank, small enough to put the whole thing in her mouth at once. Before she could think about it too much, heart racing, she shoved the meat into her mouth and bit down. It was softer than she was expecting, and she chewed it quickly, warm salt blood filling her mouth, and swallowed. She imagined its heat filling her belly, imagined courage glowing in her like fire. She cut another piece, then, feeling half-drunk with blood and the sudden strange thrill of forbidden meat, picked up the skinned carcass, sank her teeth deep, and tore the flesh away.

This is what I was made to do. She almost wished the *karanja* would see her now, blood-smeared and fierce. They would have no doubt she was meant to join them, meant to live their life and no other.

She managed two more bites before her stomach seized. She dropped the carcass, vomited until there was nothing left, and scrubbed her fur as best she could with handfuls of grass before she returned to the trail.

What I was made to do, she thought with disgust. Was she bound to fail every test?

The third snare was empty, and she hated herself for feeling suddenly glad. With a sigh that was half a growl, she cut the noose and threw the sticks into the grass.

回 ۞ 回

A full white moon rose over the village. Leya took another cup of honey-beer, letting the sweetness wash away the last sour tang from the back of her throat. The village rainspeaker, his fur rubbed with red ochre, had finished tying a length of twine to Ayanna and Jasiri's wrists, binding them about an arm's length apart. The longer the tie lasted, the better, though most didn't make it through more than a day or so. Now the males, young and old, were singing them to their hut, carrying spears aloft, calling out ribald encouragement to the young groom. When they reached the hut, they drove their spears, points up, into the ground around it, and they would leave calabashes of beer and porridge outside the door at intervals through the night, to help him keep his strength. Leya thought Jasiri looked a little scared as they went inside.

Leya slipped back to her own hut, remembering the practice spear she'd left outside. She couldn't help smiling as she picked it up; it looked like a toy now, something she'd played with as a cub. Whether she passed or failed initiation, she would have no use for it now. She snapped it in two and added the pieces to the pile of firewood.

She was on her way back to the fire-circle when she heard the young lionesses talking.

"It'll be Bahati next," one said.

Leya stopped, keeping to the shadows between the huts. They hadn't seen her.

"I hope not," another said, "unless it's me."

A third giggled. "You know the only one he wants."

"The one he can't have." A low sound like a snort. "You'd think he'd know better."

"He's been in love with Leya since they were cubs. He's never looked at anybody else."

"Not that we haven't tried."

"You're just mad that you practically pushed your breasts in his face and he acted like you were just saying good morning."

"He'd better enjoy hers while she still has them."

"You think he has?"

"They're always off alone somewhere. He says he's helping her practice."

Laughter. "Maybe he's practicing too."

The conversation moved on, but Leya stayed where she

was, unable to move, unable to think. She stared into her half-empty cup, the lionesses' voices echoing in her head long after they'd left.

He's been in love with Leya since they were cubs.

It couldn't be true. Of course it wasn't true. Those baboons would gossip at anything. She'd tell Bahati, and they'd laugh about it together, that anyone could think…

"Leya?"

Bahati. She jerked her head up so quickly the liquid in her cup sloshed over her hand.

"I can get some more," he said.

"No—I've had plenty." Too much, maybe, though the buzzing in her head was more than the beer. She would tell him right away, and they could laugh about it and move on.

But if they were right—

Of course not. It was silly. He'd known the path she was following since they were little. Yaa's whiskers, he'd carved spears for her. Why would he help her, if he wanted her for his wife?

Bahati was staring at her. "Leya? Are you all right?"

"I'm fine." She hated those girls for ruining these last hours she had with Bahati, for putting such stupid thoughts in her head to spoil things between them. "Just—warm. That's all."

"Come with me, then. I wanted to show you something anyway."

They're always off alone somewhere.

Leya told the voices in her head to shut up and followed Bahati out of the noise and light of the village, into the cool quiet of the veld. Monkeys called to each other in the distance, and crickets and cicadas thrummed in the grass. The familiar sounds soothed her startled nerves, and she felt herself relax as they reached the kopje and climbed onto the rocks, just as they always had. A star-dusted sky stretched over them. Dip a calabash in that, she thought, and it would make you dizzier than beer.

"I found something a while ago," Bahati said. "I thought you might want it back before you leave."

From a wide crevice in the rock, he took out a crude wooden box, its surface rough and lid askew. "Remember what's in here?"

It looked familiar... She frowned, trying to remember, then smiled when Bahati lifted off the lid. "My bead collection."

She hadn't seen it for years. She'd found a few beads as a cub and begged others as bridal necklaces were being strung. There was one for good harvests, three for long life, two for lasting love, and one for a sturdy home. Bahati had made the box, back when he was first teaching himself to carve.

"Not enough for a necklace," Bahati mused, producing a bone needle and a thinner version of the twine the rain-speaker had used to tie Ayanna and Jasiri together. "But let's see..." He picked up one of the beads. "This one's for lots of zebra."

"Oh, is it?"

"Yes. These are special." He picked up another. "This one's for your spear always going where you mean it to. This one's so you can get honey without bees stinging you..."

"What about ants?"

"Doesn't work for ants, sorry. Those are rare." He strung the beads one by one, tying knots carefully between them. "Can't have these rattling around, or you'll scare off the herds." He picked up the last bead, rolling in the center of his palm a moment, thinking. "And this one's for being happy."

"Just that?"

He smiled. "Just that."

"I don't get to be invisible or turn into a elephant or something?"

"If you're happy, it won't matter if you can't do things like that." He tied the last knot.

"Where'd you learn to string beads?"

He shrugged. "If you keep quiet and keep your eyes open, you learn a lot of things. Hold out your arm."

She held her right arm out, palm up, and he tied the bracelet around her wrist, tight enough to stay in place but not so tight it would chafe her fur. He knotted it twice, his fingers brushing the inside of her wrist, then took her hand gently in both of his. "Leya..."

The sudden seriousness of his voice set her heart pounding. *Don't,* she thought. She wanted to tell him now, all at once, all in one breath before he could speak again.

In the village they say you're in love with me. It's silly, isn't it? Because you should know better. You've always known I can't be anything but your friend. Isn't that enough?

"Promise me something?" Bahati asked, still holding her hand, his voice low.

She nodded, not trusting her voice. His hands were warm against hers. She felt that same sense of safety, and something else under it, excitement and fear like wings flapping hard and fast.

"Promise me you won't let anyone make you into anything you don't want to be."

She barely heard his words and wasn't even sure exactly what he meant. But he was looking at her so intently, his eyes so serious and wise and sincere... "I promise."

They walked slowly back to the village. As they reached the first of the huts, Bahati took her hand again, touching one of the beads. "I forgot to tell you—this one's also for sleeping well tonight. And this one's for luck tomorrow."

"I never thought beads could have so many meanings."

He grinned. "I told you they were special." And before she could say anything else, good night or thank you or goodbye, he turned and loped off to his hut, his golden body lit for a moment by the dying bridal fire, then lost in the shadows and the night.

She'd been told to meet Masika at dawn at the *karanja's* tents, but after her third dream of being late and finding the tents gone or being dismissed by Masika without even having a chance at whatever the test was, Leya finally got up and slipped out of her hut while it was still dark. It was better to leave, anyway, while her mother was still asleep. She had enough voices in her head to try to silence without adding her mother's real one to the group.

She wished she had some idea how to prepare. Was it a test of strength? Endurance? Something else? She only hoped it wouldn't involve eating raw meat, not with her stomach churning already. She reached the tents and climbed up on a rock to wait.

It seemed to take about four or five days for the sun to come up. She watched the tents go from deep crimson-black in the darkness to dark orangeish-red in the half-light, then at last to bright red ochre as the sun rose from the edge of the earth.

She wondered which one was Masika's. The tents all looked the same, with no difference in size or color or decoration to mark the leader's.

"Leya."

She jumped. The voice had come from behind her, and she turned to see Masika standing in full regalia.

"Come with me," Masika said.

Heart racing, Leya followed. Masika led her out into the veld, off any trails Leya knew, until the red tents were specks in the distance. Leya was just starting to wonder whether

31

the test might be how far she would walk without questioning where they were going or how far, when the *karanjala* stopped.

Leya looked around. There was nothing important or unusual about the spot that she could see, nothing but waving blond grass, a few scrubby bushes, and an ant hill or two.

Ants. *Yaa's whiskers, it's ants after all.* Her mouth went dry.

"I am told that you wish to become a huntress, Leya. Is that your wish, or someone else's for you?"

Leya tried to swallow. "It's mine."

"Very well." Masika produced a tiny box with a sliding lid, made of dark, polished wood, small enough to fit easily in Leya's palm when she handed it over. "This is your task, then. Bring me a thousand ants, and you will be *nakaranja*."

"A thousand ants." Leya looked back at the box.

"You have until sunset. If you cannot return by then, do not come to our tents again." Without waiting for acknowledgment, Masika turned and strode away through the long grass, each step as easy and sure as if she were following a trail she'd walked every day of her life.

Leya slid the box open. It was even smaller inside; the wood was thick. Would it even hold a thousand ants?

She clenched her jaw, chose the closest anthill, and plucked a stiff blade of grass.

By the time the sun had climbed the sky and stood at the very top, Leya was biting back tears so hard she could taste blood. No matter how fast she worked, every time she slid open the lid to scrape a few more ants in, a few more crawled out. They weren't as big as the ones she was used to, but they were faster, and they bit twice as hard. At first she thought she might get used to the bites, that the pain might fade into the background as she got closer to completing her task. But she was no closer than she'd been when she started, and she had several ants that seemed to be trapped under her skirt and didn't need the encouragement of honey to find tender flesh to bite.

Part of her wanted to throw the box as far as she could, just to throw *something*. She forced herself to take a deep breath instead. She didn't need to waste time looking for the box on top of what was seeming like an impossible task to begin with.

Leya slapped ants off her arms, getting a few more angry bites in retaliation, and sat down a few paces away to try to think. Giving the ants a chance to calm down a bit wouldn't hurt either.

Maybe it was supposed to be impossible. Maybe Masika wanted to see how she would handle failing. Maybe she was losing face the longer she tried, instead of accepting the test as beyond her reach and going back with an empty box.

Leya sighed and turned the box over in her hands. It was nicely made, though plain. Bahati would have carved it to make it beautiful, maybe a pattern of ants or the design of a thorn-tree. She slid it open, then shut, idly, as if the motion would unlock something in her mind. She ran her finger along the inside of the box and tried to figure out how many ants would fit inside if she could pack them in one on top of the other, as if they were already dead.

Maybe that was it. Maybe she was supposed to crush them or kill them somehow, and then stuff them into the box. But even then it didn't look big enough.

Leya said the strongest curse she knew softly, then louder. No one here to hear her except the stupid ants, anyway.

It wasn't supposed to be this way. She was supposed to prove herself, supposed to do something strong and glorious, something that would wring the strength out of her body and leave her shaken and exhausted and victorious. Instead, her head ached from the sun, her hand was starting to swell, and the bites that weren't still stinging had started to itch.

She hadn't said "bring me a thousand ants in the box," Leya realized suddenly. Was the box part a trick? Was she supposed to carry them back some other way?

I could just sit on the thing and carry back a thousand all over me, she thought with disgust. *Right into their tents, too.*

The sun began its descent. Leya sat by the anthill, the box next to her foot, knees drawn up, chin on her arms. She longed for shade but didn't want to leave until she found a way to complete the task. Instead, she gazed dully at the ant hill, watching lines come and go, half-dozing from the heat and her exhausted frustration, watching the ants crawl down the hill, crawl up the hill, disappear inside, imagining the cooler dark inside, a low hum of ant-noise, the hidden chambers of eggs to guard and tend...

Eggs.

Leya jerked awake and grabbed the box. It wouldn't hold a thousand ants. Would it hold a thousand eggs? Did an ant hill even have a thousand eggs in it?

The sun was low into late afternoon, but it wasn't setting yet. Leya frantically searched for something to dig with and found a flat bit of wood. She hesitated in front of the hill, wondering how many times someone could be bitten before their head swelled up like a melon and they died a horrible choking death.

Time to find out.

The ants swarmed up her arm, her shoulder, her neck. One bit her ear, another her lip, but the bites weren't as bad as the crawling, everywhere at once, every crevice of her body, and knowing that bites were sure to come. She focused on the anthill and dug deeper, moving the grit away carefully, not wanting to bury the tunnels and chambers she was looking for.

She spotted a worker ant carrying something white and

caught it on the piece of wood, turning the wood around and around as the ant ran along it. It was tiny, but even if there were a thousand inside, and even if she could find them, it still didn't look like they would all fit. The box wasn't made to hold a thousand of anything. It would fit a dozen ants comfortably if they were small, with room to move around. Maybe just one ant, if it were the queen.

The queen.

You idiot cub, it's a riddle.

She heard her own voice as if it were outside her head.

A queen could lay a thousand eggs in her lifetime. Maybe more. If she could find the queen, she'd have a thousand ants in one, the way a seed held the chance of a thousand melons.

She dug deeper. The afternoon light turned gold, then amber, then orange. The bottom edge of the sun was a whisker's-breadth from the horizon when she found the queen, twice the size of the other ants. Gently she tipped the ant into the box and slid the lid closed.

Leya stood, swaying on her feet, her legs shaking from being crouched so long. The sky was turning crimson. She squinted into the distance, found the specks of the *karanja's* tents, and ran.

Masika waited, still and silent, as Leya slowed to a stop. Leya's chest ached, her head throbbed, and she was glad she'd eaten nothing, or it would have ended up at the *karanjala's* feet. Instead she held out the box, the only sound her blood in her ears and her ragged, desperate breaths.

Masika's gaze flicked down to the box, though no other part of her moved. She slid the lid open with her thumb, slid it closed. She looked up then, and held Leya's gaze as surely and completely as she had when Leya was a cub.

And smiled.

Masika spoke as if she addressed an entire village instead of a single gasping lioness on fire with ant bites. "The queen carries a thousand ants within her. What you carry within you, Leya, we will learn together."

Masika turned then to the tents and cried out with a sound that was somewhere between a hyena's whoop and a monkey's scream, a sound that seemed impossible from a lion's chest. The other karanja emerged then; a half-dozen or so, Leya thought, though her vision was wavering.

Masika shoved Leya hard, forcing her to stagger a step forward, and called out. "*Nakaranja!*"

The others echoed it. A sob choked its way out of Leya's throat. They had surrounded her; they were lifting her. The red sky filled her vision, and she was drinking it, hot and salt and sweet as blood, filling her up, singing in her veins. She was flying through it, soaring through it, higher and higher, the swift, sharp-winged bird of her soul free, finally free.

That night, they held the village ceremony that marked her as *nakaranja*. Masika stood before Leya's mother and slowly drew thick lines of red ochre from the corners of Naimah's eyes to the curve of her jaw, as they did in mourning. The Leya the village knew would never return. She was dead, and now she dwelled in the in-between of the *nakaranja*, the initiate, until the day she killed on her own and would be reborn as a huntress. The *karanja* pressed their palms into the paste and rubbed Leya all over, staining her fur as one did for the dead.

Naimah watched them silently, her tears blending into the red streaks, sending thin tendrils of color down her jaw and throat.

Leya looked for Bahati but never saw him.

CHAPTER 2

Leya crouched in the mud at the riverbank and held the calabash in the sluggish current. It was full, and had been full for some time, but the water felt good on her sore arms and the cool mud soothed the raw pads of her feet. They would expect her back soon, but she allowed herself just one breath more, and then another, and then another.

It was her ninth day among the *karanja*. Nine days of carrying water, sharpening knives and spears, taking down the tents, putting up the tents, and any other menial task they could find for her. She hadn't held a weapon except to sharpen it or clean it or polish it with beeswax. She hadn't touched meat except to cut it in thin strips—though never quite thin enough—to prepare it for drying. While the others gorged themselves on the meat, she was given the tasteless flatbread, her only consolation a thin smear of honey that managed to make the bread itself taste even more bland. And though nearly every twilight a group of three or four would go out among the herds to hunt, Leya was always left behind.

Sighing, she pulled the full calabash up from the river, tipping out a frog that had wandered in. The only new skill she'd mastered since initiation was finally being strong and steady enough to carry the full calabash on her head, as her mother had so easily done.

I might as well have stayed at home, she thought, trudging back. All she was doing were the same tasks any lioness in the village could do, and at least there, the others would be doing them too. Here, when they weren't hunting, the *karanja* she'd so idolized and envied seemed to spend most of their time sleeping—and ordering her around.

Leya reached the tents and set the calabash carefully on the ground. Once she'd made the mistake of letting some of the water slosh out when she set it down, and she'd had to go back to the river and start over.

"Leya!"

Leya recognized Thembe's voice. She had been the first *karanja* other than Masika that Leya knew by sight, thanks to her pale fur. Soon enough, though, Leya learned she was also the most demanding of the group. The others told her to do things; Thembe commanded her. When something wasn't right, the others told her to do it again or differently; Thembe's voice made it clear that Leya was too weak or too slow or too stupid to ever do it properly.

Leya felt her jaw clench as she trotted over to where the pale lioness lay stretched on a grass mat in the shade. "Yes, sister?"

It left a sour taste in her mouth to call Thembe that, but *nakaranja* were not allowed to address their elders by anything else. Certainly she couldn't call Thembe any of the names she thought up on all the long, dusty, aching walks to the river and back.

"Water," Thembe said, not even looking at her.

"Yes, sister."

Leya found the drinking-gourd sitting by their fire-pit, carried the gourd to the calabash, filled it, and took it to Thembe. As usual, Thembe did not even bother to nod acknowledgment of the task. She drank without looking at Leya and shoved the empty gourd back at her. Leya's hands tightened around it, but she said nothing.

Sometimes at night, lying on her grass mat outside the tents, listening to Thembe's snoring, she thought of how she'd expected things to be. It was a bitter pastime. She'd thought that moment of acceptance she'd felt at initiation would last, that she would feel part of something big and important that stretched long before her birth and would go on even after her death. But it was hard to feel that when you spent half the day gathering dried dung from the veld for the cook-fires.

"Leya!"

She didn't cry, not even at night, afraid the others might hear. But it didn't keep her from wanting to.

She settled on her haunches by the fire and added more fuel to the flames, spreading the coals to keep the heat low and even. Above the fire, strips of impala meat cooked slowly, droplets of fat sizzling and popping as they fell into the flames.

Leya breathed through her half-open mouth, letting the scent back where she could taste it. She glanced around the camp. The others were sleeping or lounging. There were six other *karanja*, which meant a dozen eyes that could be watching, but for once no one was looking in her direction.

She looked back at the meat. It would burn her mouth, but it would be worth it. She eyed the smallest strip, measuring the distance to reach. It was her own little hunt, her own ambush, waiting for just the right moment...

"Leya!"

She jumped, her arm hitting the greenwood rack and tipping the whole thing into the coals. The meat flamed, then charred as she grabbed at the rack and set it upright again.

Thembe stood over her, arms crossed over her scarred chest, a satisfied smirk twisting her mouth. Then she walked off without a word, hips swinging, and sprawled on her mat again.

Leya bit back a dozen distinct curses, rose silently, and went to cut more meat. She had just refilled the rack when Thembe called for her again.

"Water."

As Leya walked to the calabash, she imagined herself pouring the entire thing over Thembe's head, soaking her sleek to the skin. She filled the gourd and took it back. Thembe took it from her, looked her steadily in the eye, brought the rim of the gourd to her mouth—then held the gourd at arm's length and poured the water onto the ground.

Leya's claws dug into her palms. She could hear blood in her ears, feel her nostrils flaring with every jerking breath.

Thembe watched her, grinning, looking at her as if Leya were a cub tugging on her tail, an amusing nuisance to be cuffed aside.

"You—" Words flew out of her head, useless in Leya's sudden rage. Still Thembe kept the same mocking expression, waiting with her head cocked, hands on hips.

"You have something to say to me—*sister*?" Thembe asked.

Leya realized the camp had fallen silent around them, not the usual lazy quiet of the daytime but a tense, waiting silence, the space between lightning and thunder. The only sound left was the hissing and crackling of the fire.

Slowly, slowly Leya unclenched her hands. Her lungs filled, emptied, filled again. Her voice sounded distant in her ears. "No, sister. I have nothing to say."

"Good." Thembe dropped the drinking-gourd and kicked it toward Leya. "Then bring me more water."

Leya bent down and picked up the gourd. Her hand closed tightly around it, then tighter, until she felt it crack. Slowly she straightened up and met Thembe's hard gaze with her own. "No."

Thembe's gaze did not waver. "What did you say, cub?"

Leya dropped the pieces of the gourd into the dust. "I said no. *Sister*. I didn't pass initiation to be your wife. Get your own water."

Leya turned to walk away and nearly ran face-first into Masika standing behind her. Masika gazed down at her, eyes like smooth stones. "Leya."

Leya swallowed, courage seeping from her as fast as the water had drained into the dry ground.

"Hold out your hands," Masika said.

Leya held them out, palms up, wondering if the *karanjala* was going to strike her across them. She stared at the ground and waited.

Something long and thin balanced itself across her palms. Leya closed her hands around it instinctively. The shaft of a spear.

She looked up. It was Thembe now who stood before her, and for the first time, her smile was sincere. "Took you long enough, sister," she said. Then the white lioness laughed, took her spear from Leya's hands, and pulled her into an embrace so tight she could hardly breathe.

Leya's tenth day as a *nakaranja* dawned brighter and wider and more beautiful than any she'd ever seen. It was as if every huntress had worn a mask, and now she saw the true faces beneath. The huntresses who had lounged in the camp while Leya did all the work now slipped easily back into the usual routines, dividing tasks according to each lioness' strengths, careful not to let too much of the tedious labor fall too often on any individual.

"It's been a long time since we had a *nakaranja*," Thembe told her as they carried water back from the river. "It was a nice rest while it lasted."

Though she was still getting used to the others' company, and they to hers, she at last felt the beginnings of the companionship she'd longed for. She'd never had sisters, and the friendships that formed among the village girls had always seemed shallow and strange to her from the outside, but now she began to understand. Leya was the youngest of the group by far, and the others became, to her, older sisters and aunts. Only two still remained apart in her mind.

One was their rainspeaker, Zhenga, who was the oldest

of their pride. Leya hadn't even known a lioness could be a rainspeaker, but Thembe whispered to her that Zhenga had walked with Kamara the Huntress herself, in the other world, and learned from her. This rainspeaker didn't stay painted with red ochre as the village one did—likely because the color would stand out too much and risk spoiling the hunt—but she did keep the twin tearstreaks of mourning all the time, to honor both the lives of their prey and the spirits of the *karanja* who had walked these trails before them. Zhenga went on every hunt, though she stayed back until the kill was made. Then she came to perform the simple rites that ensured the prey's spirit left its body and went to the next world. If this were neglected, Thembe explained, the spirit might stay in the meat and make trouble for those who ate it. Leya thought back to the gazelle fawn and wondered. Maybe it hadn't had a spirit yet, the way new cubs didn't at first.

The other she couldn't think of as a sister, at least not yet and maybe not ever, was Masika. To Leya, the *karanjala*, even without the feather mane and jewelry, was less of a real lioness and more a living goddess, a part of Kamara made flesh and bone, to watch and listen to and learn from. Whenever Masika spoke, Leya became her cub-self again, caught in admiration and wonder.

And Thembe, of course, was special, too. Beginning on that ninth night, Leya had been allowed to sleep in Thembe's tent. The pale lioness was what the *karanja* called her second mother, the one who had finally kindled the fire in her to stand up for herself, and as such, Thembe was responsible for most of Leya's training from then on.

At first, it was somewhat disorienting to have been insulted and provoked by Thembe one day and embraced and welcomed as a daughter the next. For a time, Leya found herself nervous and uncertain around her, as if Thembe were speaking with someone else's voice and might suddenly go back to her own and begin ordering her around again. But Thembe's laughter now was never at Leya's expense—or if it was, as when Leya made her first attempt at gathering honey and had to jump into a water hole to escape the bees, it was the laughter of one who remembered her own days as an initiate, and Leya found she had no trouble laughing along with her.

It wasn't just Thembe's coat that set her apart from the others; she was stockier, rounder in the hips and belly than the others, and she moved with a kind of defiant grace. Watching her, Leya thought of a mother elephant, strong and steady and wise—at least, until an evening at the fire-circle when Thembe started telling ribald jokes about various village *aumahs*. Leya was horrified at first, but Thembe shoved her playfully. "It's all right to laugh, Leya. They're only men. Though some more than others."

It was Thembe who told her that though the *karanja* could not take mates, they sometimes took lovers among the villagers. Leya had never even thought about the possibility. She realized, with some embarrassment, that she'd always imagined the huntresses as so devoted to the chase and the kill that it drove everything else from their minds—and their bodies. When she tried to stammer her way through an explanation of that to Thembe, the white lioness had laughed. They were packing the dried strips of zebra meat into baskets, to take to a village soon.

"It's a lot harder to cut things out of your head than out from the body," Thembe said. "We're still women, no matter how we live."

"Do you... have one?"

"Oh, no. I like to look, but I haven't seen any worth the trouble so far. Though there's three of them right now that would love for me to change my mind. An *aumah*, an *aumah*'s first son, and a rainspeaker."

"A *rainspeaker*? But I thought they didn't—do any of that."

"This one does. Or would, anyway. Every time he sees me, he compares me to the snow that graces the sacred mountain." She shook her head. "No sense in that one at all."

"So the males don't mind that..." Leya gestured vaguely at her chest.

"Some seem to like it better. I don't understand it, but don't ask me to explain what goes through their minds. Some will treat you like you're a man, talk to you all day about the hunt, and never look at you twice. Others like the *karanja* more than their women. Probably because we don't live with them."

Leya hesitated, deciding whether to ask, whether she really wanted to know. "What about Masika? Does she... see anyone?"

Thembe shrugged. "If she does, she keeps quiet about it." She paused. "I should tell you this, though, so you know. You'll go with us to the village when all this is ready. If someone catches your eye, I won't tell you what you can and can't do—but there are three things you have to remember when we're there."

"All right." Leya said it lightly, as if she were paying more attention to laying strips of meat over the fire than to the conversation, but her heart raced as she waited for Thembe to go on.

"You can have any of them you like. Even a rainspeaker if you like him." She chuckled. "But never lie with anyone more than once in a night. Never mind what they say. Once is safe enough, but past that you're taking your chances. Understand?"

Leya nodded.

"Second. If any male ever tries to force you—or if he does—they're no more to you than the zebra or the kudu or the pigs. Kill him. If you can't kill him, tell us who he is, and we will. No man touches a *karanja* except by her will, or he dies. That goes for rainspeakers and *aumahs* and Yaa himself." Thembe's eyes were bright flames.

Leya swallowed. "What's the third?"

"The most important. We give men our bodies. Not our hearts. If we could cut those away and still live, we would. Take a man in every village and a few rangers too if you want, and enjoy every night with every one. But never forget what you are. Your heart is bound with this land, with the herds, with your sisters, and with the hunt. Keep it close to you as your knife, and give it to no one."

Leya agreed solemnly, though she couldn't imagine needing to heed any of Thembe's warnings. That night, before falling asleep, she tried to imagine what her lover might look like, what type she would choose if she could piece him together just as she wanted. But all she kept seeing in her mind was a young, strong, golden-maned male who looked suspiciously like Bahati—probably, she figured, because he'd been the only one she'd ever spent much time looking at. What would he say to her? Where would they go? And afterward, what would that be like? She fell asleep wondering, and dreamed of a whole village full of males lined up and waiting for her, all of them with Bahati's deep, sincere, laughing eyes.

回 ‍۞ 回

Thembe nudged her out of sleep while it was still dark. "Leya. Get up."

"What is it?"

Thembe lit an oil lamp, adding more smoke than light to the inside of the tent. "Time to hunt."

Leya was fully awake at the words. "And—I'm going with you?"

"Of course you're going with us." Thembe took out a

small basket of earth and started rubbing it into her pale fur. "When I was a cub, I would have loved a reason to get this dirty. Now all I can think about is how long it'll take to get clean again."

Leya eyed Thembe's spear at its place by her sleeping-mat, always within arm's reach. "What weapon do I take?"

"None. Not even your knife. You're not killing; you're just watching. It'll be that way the first few times, until you make your own weapons. If there's any trouble, run. I'll look after you."

Leya thought about asking what kind of trouble there could be, and then decided she didn't need to know.

The night felt hushed at first, as if the land itself knew that the *karanja* were awake and tracking their prey. As Leya followed the others through the long grass, bit by bit she heard more, saw more, smelled more, until she realized the night was as busy and alive as the day. She concentrated on moving as Thembe had taught her, slowly, smoothly, the pads of her feet touching the earth and pressing only lightly before taking the next step. For all her care, she still seemed to move twice as loudly as any of the others, but no one glared at her or sent her away, so she figured she was being quiet enough.

She heard their prey before she saw it: the soft grunts and stamps of a small herd of grazing wildebeest. They were close enough that Leya could hear their teeth tearing the grass, their wet chewing, the quiet thumps of their hooves and the small gusts of their breathing. She had never been this close to anything so large and strong.

She felt Thembe at her side, felt the lioness put a hand lightly on her arm. Slowly the two of them made a wide circle around the herd, moving back then and working their way up a rise of earth, low enough that they wouldn't be seen, but high enough to watch the hunt play out. There was only a sliver of moon out, sleek and sharp as a claw, but it was more than enough for Leya to see three of the others carefully moving into position.

Masika and Nanji, the *karanja*'s most skilled tracker, circled quietly into position to either side of the herd, waiting there for the prey to be driven to them. The third lioness crept closer to the wildebeest, bit by bit, each step deliberate and cautious. She seemed to have singled one out, and then, still keeping low and in slow, fluid movements, she put out her hand to signal the others, fist closed, then open, then the first and second fingers held apart.

Leya glanced at Thembe, confused.

"She's telling them to watch the male with a limp in his right hind leg," Thembe whispered, her mouth pressed nearly into Leya's ear.

Leya looked back at the herd, amazed at how close they'd gotten. She found Masika and Nanji's light coats among the long grass, and the third lioness' darker one.

And then she saw something else, a flicker of movement farther in the distance, shadow on shadow. At first she thought it was one of the wildebeest or some other prey moving through the night, but then it stood up and dropped back into a crouch and started to move away, and she knew it wasn't anything on four legs.

She was just about to say something to Thembe about it when one of the wildebeest suddenly startled and stamped, leaping forward. Panic swept through the herd like wind bending the grass. At first the wildebeest were confused, not sure which way to run, but instinct took over quickly, and the herd moved as a dark mass through the night, bucking and snorting and kicking anything that came too close. Leya tried to look for the one the *karanja* had chosen, but in the next instant, the herd turned and headed straight for Thembe and Leya.

Thembe grabbed Leya's wrist as the herd thundered toward them. "Stay close!"

Leya ran through the night, following Thembe's lighter form amid the darkness and the dust. They cut across the bulk of the herd, dodging stragglers, though once Leya brushed one close enough to feel its wet breath on her side. At last the night fell quiet again, though she could still hear the herd in the distance, grunting and snorting, still wary and anxious.

Leya caught up to Thembe. The white lioness was slitting the throat of a calf that had gotten separated from its mother. Leya could smell the blood soaking into the dry ground.

"Not much," Thembe grumbled, "but it's better than nothing."

"Will they try again?"

Thembe shook her head. "The herd's too stirred up now. They won't calm down enough to get close again tonight."

Leya heard other voices approaching. Nanji was a sweet-hearted lioness who would do anything for her sisters, but she could also swear more fluently and vividly than anyone, male or female, Leya had ever known. Nanji shot the words like spears into the night, and Masika and the others came following.

"What spooked them?" Thembe asked, holding up the calf's carcass for the blood to drain.

"Nothing," Nanji spat. "Nothing I saw. Maybe one of the stupid things stepped on an anthill. Hope they all break their necks."

Leya thought of the figure she'd seen. The wind had been with the *karanja*, but maybe whoever—whatever—it was had been in the wrong place and been seen, or smelled, or heard. There were no villages nearby, no scent of cooking-fires on the wind or huts standing in the distance. Would another band of *karanja* have been out hunting the same herd tonight?

Leya started to ask, but Nanji spoke first. "At least we got something. Let's get back to camp and divide up everyone's two bites."

"Better two bites than going hungry," Masika said mildly. Then she glanced at Leya. "From this night, *nakaranja*, learn that sometimes you must change your chosen prey in the middle of the hunt. It isn't failure," she added, with a glance at Nanji, "as long as your belly's full at the end."

Masika led them back to the tents. Once Leya thought she heard something in the grass, very close by, but when she looked, there was nothing there.

They slept late the next day, rousing when the sun was high just long enough to roast the calf and eat it down to the cracked bones. After that, they slept again, through the heat of the afternoon.

No one said anything about the night before, and Leya figured no one else had seen anything. Maybe she hadn't either. She was new to nighttime hunting; maybe it had only been a particular kind of shadow or trick of the moonlight or the wind in the grass.

Leya was on her way back from gathering firewood in the early evening, wondering if they would hunt again that night, when she stepped on something small and hard, like a pebble digging into her footpad. She started to kick it aside, then saw it wasn't a stone, but a bead.

She picked it up. It was an oval wooden bead, meticulously smoothed and polished, and carved with a design so small she had to squint to make it out: a line of ants winding around and around in a spiral.

She knew only one person who could carve something so delicately—and all at once she felt certain who had been out in the veld the night before.

She closed her hand around the bead, went into her tent, and looked at the carving again. Then, glad there was no one to see her, she opened her palm and sniffed the wood, closing her eyes.

Bahati. Her heart raced at the scent. He wouldn't actually come here, would he? He had to know better than that. All the males knew not to approach the *karanja*'s tents.

She rolled the bead in her palm. It was small, and it was light. Throw it—maybe with a cub's slingshot—and it could fly far. It was no coincidence it had shown up outside her tent.

Did that mean he'd been watching them, to know which tent was hers? Her stomach gave an odd fluttering lurch, not quite embarrassment and not quite anxiety. She hadn't thought Bahati could do something so bold. She wished she could see him, talk to him…

She looked back down at the bead, and the dust cleared in her mind. The ants… Was it a message? There were few landmarks in this part of the veld, but they weren't far from the anthills where she'd passed initiation. She remembered where they were; would he have found out somehow?

There was only one way to be sure. Leya tucked the bead under a corner of her sleeping-mat and waited for nightfall.

Thankfully, there was no hunt that night. She said a brief prayer of thanks to Yaa that her second mother slept heavily, then used all her knowledge of silent movement to leave the grouping of tents and head out into the veld. For one terrifying moment, she almost got lost, but then her memories of trails returned, and she found the right place. One of the anthills had been trampled, but the other still stood, and she gave it a wide berth as she surveyed the area. Then the wind shifted, and with it came a soft, familiar musk.

Leya turned. Bahati smiled slowly, his eyes mirroring the moonlight.

"I guess you found it," he said quietly. "I didn't know if you'd understand."

"What are you doing here?" She hadn't meant it to sound so accusing, but she couldn't take it back, even when she saw him flinch at the words.

"I just... wanted to see you. That's all."

"We could both get in trouble. If they see you anywhere near the tents—"

"Leya." He gave her a teasing, exasperated smile. "I'm not *that* stupid."

"Stupid enough." Her anger surprised her, but she couldn't keep it back. "We lost a hunt because of you. Somebody could have been hurt. I could have been."

"What?"

"Last night, in the veld."

He frowned. "That wasn't me."

"The wildebeest herd?"

He shook his head.

"Oh." Her irritation drained away, left her standing with nothing else ready to say. She found herself fingering the beads on the bracelet he'd given her.

Bahati glanced down at it and smiled. His expression was so familiar, so much a part of home and comfort, that she fought to keep tears back.

"I've missed you," he said quietly.

Leya swallowed. "I've missed you, too. How are things at home?"

Bahati shrugged. "The same."

"Mother...?"

"She's fine. Though she doesn't look at me much. I think she was hoping..." He shrugged again. "It'll take time, I guess.

Maybe she'll be better by the time you come back for the first time."

"It might be a while." *Nakaranja* couldn't return to their villages until they became *karanja*, to keep their previous lives from putting up barriers to the new. She wouldn't be *karanja* until her first solo kill, and so far she hadn't even tried to make the point of a spear. Wearing the zebra hide seemed a lifetime away.

Leya looked back at Bahati, then looked away. When had his gaze gotten so intense? It was like looking into the sun, like Masika's gaze, only this seemed to ask even more of her, while making all the thoughts in her head scatter into the starlit sky.

They walked the trails, as they had for years together. Before, they'd always talked about dreams and wishes, things Leya would do when she became one of the huntresses. Now they walked in silence, and Leya tried desperately to think of something to say that felt common and safe. "How's Ayanna?"

Bahati gave an embarrassed grin. "Looking like a ripe melon. They say it might be twins."

Leya thought of the bridal necklace she'd almost made, all the beads for cubs strung together, and chuckled. "Well, it's a good start." She glanced at Bahati. "What?"

"Nothing. It's just good to finally see you smile. I was afraid maybe… maybe you weren't happy."

Bahati settled down against the base of a thorn-tree. Leya hesitated. For years they'd tumbled and wrestled like cubs, in a physical affection that was both innocent and completely comfortable. She wanted very much to be that way again, and yet…

She was being silly. This was Bahati. They were friends. That was all. She sat down, leaned into him, felt him put his arm around her. There. Just like old times, easy and warm and safe.

Except it wasn't.

His last words suddenly broke through. "You were afraid I wasn't happy? Why wouldn't I be?"

"I don't know. No reason. I just wanted to be sure."

Silence fell over them gently. She rested her head against his chest, felt him breathing, buried her nose in his fur, breathed in musk and sunlight and earth and fresh-carved wood, sweet and clean. Her heart pounded. This wasn't how she'd always felt before. She wasn't sure whether she liked it. Once, when they were all cubs, she and the other males had dared each other to see how close they would stand to the edge of a low cliff. This was that same feeling, the same dizzy rush, the same sense that she was about to tumble over, nothing to catch her, nothing to save her, just a fall that would somehow go on forever.

She looked up at him, the line of his jaw, the soft haze of his mane, almost full now. Before she realized what she was doing, she reached up and touched his cheek, tracing his jawline back with her fingertips, stroking his mane. It was as soft as it looked.

"Leya." He'd never said it that way before, like a sigh, like the last word of a prayer.

She couldn't believe what she was doing. She felt like she'd drunk honey-beer until the earth tilted below her, only everything felt strangely sharper, clearer, stronger, the moonlight bright as day.

She nuzzled his throat. For a moment she felt his heartbeat against her muzzle, racing as fast as her own.

Bahati lowered his head, his whiskers brushing hers. Without meaning to, without plan, without thought she stroked her tongue over his chin. Then she felt his on her mouth—and jerked back with a gasp.

A moment passed. She knew she had to look away, had to get back to herself somehow, out of his gaze, out of everything it made her want that she didn't understand. She pulled away, stood up, walked a few paces away, stared up into the sky, counted stars until her heart slowed back to normal. The night felt sharply cool after his warmth next to her, and she hugged herself, arms tight over her breasts. She couldn't name what she was feeling; it was bigger than anything she'd known. It was too big, too complicated, too much. She felt tears sting her eyes, though she wasn't sure why she was crying.

"Leya." Gentle, calm, safe, and his warmth next to her again. "I've tried to tell you for years. But I'd be a fool to tell you now, when it's too late, when it doesn't matter."

He touched her arm, and she moved toward him, and he held her. She heard herself sob, a sudden heave of her chest that made him hold her tighter. His breath warmed her ear.

"Leya… I love you. I always have. I always will."

She fought to get her breath, her voice under her control again. "You shouldn't."

"I know."

"I can't."

His voice fell softer still. "I know."

She pulled away again, staggered back a few steps. She felt like putting up her hands to warn him off, to keep him away. If he touched her again, how could she go back? How could she be what she needed—wanted—to be?

Helpless rage swelled in her, and she glared at him through a blurry wash of tears. "How dare you come here."

"Leya—"

"Don't come back. Don't ever come back. Don't you dare. I can't—" Her throat closed; she fought it. "I was happy. Do you think I can't be happy without you? Like my mother thinks—like everybody thinks I can't be happy without you? If you loved me, why did you help me? Why did you carve all those stupid spears? Didn't you know where I was going?"

Bahati drew in a slow breath, and moonlight caught the sudden shine in his eyes. "I helped you because I love you, and because all I want—all I've ever wanted—is for you to be happy. With or without me. You wanted to join the *karanja*. So that's what I wanted for you." He held out his hands. "What else was I supposed to do?"

Leya felt her tears soak through fur to the skin beneath. She reached to her wrist, found the bracelet, pulled at it hard. It was tied too tight to slip off. She blinked her eyes clear and fumbled with the knot for a moment but couldn't manage it. At last, frustrated, angry at Bahati, angry at herself, angry at everything, she brought her wrist to her mouth and bit through the twine.

Bahati stood silently, edged in blue moonlight. She crossed the space between them in two strides, grabbed his hand, and pressed the bracelet into it.

She wanted to say it deliberately, sharply, like a *karanja's* command. Instead it came out as a whisper. "Don't come back."

Then, before he could say anything in reply, before what she was keeping down within her could rise up again, she turned from him and ran into the night.

Let them cut me now, she thought, *let them give me the zebra hide to wear.*

Because when she'd given him the bracelet, for an instant she'd glimpsed his eyes, and what she'd seen in them left no doubt.

She'd made her first kill.

"And Kamara knew her sister was dying. She could see the spirit leaving her like the water left the earth. And so..." Leya paused, closed her eyes, struggled to remember. "She went to the last place where water still stood, to find a spirit to give in place of her sister. She waited there... Ten days and ten nights, until..."

The words weren't there. Leya shook her head.

"Until she felt thunder in her chest." Thembe picked up the story.

Leya nodded. "Until she felt thunder in her chest, and the elephants came like rainclouds gathering. They had a calf, not three days old, and among their kind even those not yet born have spirits strong within them."

Rain pattered on the tent overhead as Leya paused to remember the next line. The short rains had come, and each afternoon the sky opened, like a story ending the same way every time. Some parts of Leya's training could only be done outside, but learning all of Kamara's stories by heart was a task made for the rains.

"Kamara took up her spear and crept quiet and close. She..."

Thembe picked up the story in a singsong as she threaded another gazelle tooth onto the necklace she was making, then followed it with a red clay bead. "She was close enough to throw the spear when the calf's mother saw her. 'Come no closer,' the elephant mother said, 'for I know you—"

"'Come with death in your heart,'" Leya cut back in, nodding. "'I do,' Kamara said, 'but I come with fear of death, for my sister, who is half my heart, lies dying, and I will have another's spirit to give Yaa in her stead, so she might live.' And the mother saw that Kamara would not be turned away, and that death would come to her herd no matter what she did. 'Then take mine,' she told the Huntress, 'and leave my calf to live.' And she lay down and lifted her head and bared her great throat to Kamara to cut. The blood ran out for... three days?"

Thembe nodded and slipped a kudu-hoof bead onto the

necklace.

"Three days," Leya went on, "and where it ran there was always water after, even when all else had dried to hard clay. And Kamara's bravery pleased Yaa, and the spirit was worthy of Him, and from that moment Kamara's sister felt strength flow back into her, and she lived for more years than a person could count."

Thembe nodded. "Very good. I think we'll leave that one be."

Leya sighed with relief. She'd learned a dozen stories so far, and she was starting to suspect that Thembe had made up a few new ones all on her own, just to test Leya's memory.

She had learned more than just stories, though. In the weeks that had passed since the night of her first hunt, she had observed several kills and had begun to learn the particular habits and weaknesses of each type of prey. She knew the signals, now, for male and female, for left and right, front and hind, for the calves and the wounded. She could take down a tent, fold it properly, and set it back up again, and she was learning the web of trails that crisscrossed the veld, made by generations of *karanja*. She was learning where the herds moved through the turning of the year, and where the best cover was for hunting in the rains and the dry seasons. She could move as silently and as quickly now as any of them. She had learned how to forage, how to find water, how to kindle a fire, how to take honey without being stung, and she'd even sat in the midday sun for hours with blood smeared under her eyes, until she could sit absolutely still and not even twitch at the touch of a fly.

And now, at last, she was working on her first spear. She'd cut a strong, straight branch and was working now on carving away the bark, sliver by sliver, until the wood was smooth enough to fly.

She went back to work on it now while Thembe continued with the necklace. In a tradition that reminded Leya of the bridal necklaces back home, it was Thembe's place, as her second mother, to make the necklace of bone and hoof and tooth that Leya would wear once she became a full *karanja*. There would be pieces in it from kills made by every one of the others, and in the center, a bead of elephant ivory, older than Leya herself, that was the rainspeaker's contribution.

"We go to a village tomorrow," Thembe said, out of nowhere. She had a way of stating such news straight out instead of fluttering around the edges of it.

"All of us?" Leya asked.

Thembe nodded and strung another bead. "You remember what I told you?"

"I remember." She stripped another length of bark from the branch. The wood beneath smelled clean and sweet, like new grass after rain. It was the same scent that had often clung to Bahati's fur and mane when he'd been carving.

She tried to slam a lid shut on the thought, but it was like trying to fit those ants into the tiny box; you could close one up, but others crawled out.

She wondered what he was doing. Wondered if he still thought about her sometimes, in idle moments of scent and sound and memory, the way she thought of him now. Had he found someone else?

Better for him if he had. Better that he could be with someone who could give him all of herself, a whole self, and not just her body. Someone who could give him her heart, as she was forbidden to do.

"What village are we going to?" Leya asked.

"Thutiwa. It's a little bigger than yours. The women make beautiful baskets there. We'll probably trade for some."

She thought about Thembe's warnings. The thought of courting—being courted—with no obligation beyond a night was so new it was hard to imagine it happening to her. Besides, she'd gotten so used to the *karanja*'s company, to everyone's quirks and preferences and temperaments, that the thought of going among strangers was both exciting and intimidating at once. Would they do things differently, speak differently, than in Lwazi? Or would it be the same huts, the same fire-circle, the same sorts of people she'd always known, except with different faces? She was so engrossed by the possibilities, she lay awake half the night imagining what it might be like, what it would feel like to walk into a village as one of the *karanja*, where no one knew her as anything else.

At least, she tried to tell herself that was why she was awake. It had nothing to do, of course, with the tiny lump under one corner of her sleeping-mat, the one she could feel no matter how she lay, where she'd hidden the wooden bead Bahati had used to signal her. The next morning, when she rolled up her sleeping-mat, she left the bead there, pressed into the earth by the weight of her body. When they broke camp, she did not look back.

回⚙回

They came into the village of Thutiwa at sunset the next day, and Leya was struck by how much like her own it looked. As Thembe had said, it was bigger, more huts and more space between them, more families and more cubs underfoot, watching the *karanja* with wide eyes. But they built their huts the same way, the same mud and grass and wood, and the great fire in the circle had the same scent, and they spoke the same way. The only real difference Leya could see was that the lionesses here preferred clay and bone beads in their jewelry instead of the wooden ones used more often in her village.

Leya held her head high as she followed Thembe, each of them carrying a basket of dried meat. She was not a half-grown cub who'd never seen any village but her own. She was one of the huntresses now—or close enough, anyway, for the villagers. She tried to act as if she'd done this many times before, as if the meat she carried were from her own kill.

The food that evening tasted wonderful after so many days of meat and flatbread with honey, and the *karanja* feasted on long-simmered soups and stews of okra and eggplant, boiled amaranth greens with mushrooms, stuffed grouse, and baskets of fried grasshoppers and roasted dika nuts. The baked cassava wasn't as good as her mother had always made—a little more peppery than she liked—but the honey-beer was lighter and sweeter, almost fizzing on her tongue, and she didn't mind having to drink a bit more of it.

The night stretched on, and the drumming and dancing began. She couldn't help noticing that none of their drummers were as good as Bahati. Most were older males, except for one younger, with a striking mane that started the color of honey and then darkened almost to black around his shoulders. He had darker eyes, too, she saw, almost reddish-brown in the firelight. He played without Bahati's easy concentration, and when he made a mistake or lost the rhythm, he shrugged and grinned to himself and picked the beat back up again, as if it didn't matter, even when the others teased him for it. Once he caught Leya looking at him and flashed her the same quick smile, knowing and sharp. She felt her ears burn and looked away, watching the dancers instead.

When the dance ended, Thutiwa's rainspeaker, a lion with a broken tooth and a coat as light as Thembe's beneath the streaks of red ochre, invited the *karanja* to tell a story of Kamara the Huntress. To Leya's surprise, Thembe went forward and told the story, in the kind of voice Leya had never heard from her before, low and quick and somber and light as the story demanded. She told the same story Leya had just learned by heart, Kamara and the elephant, and yet to Leya it felt as if she'd never truly heard it before, as if the words were new. It felt as if Kamara might come to the fireside now, like the story had happened only the day before. It was a kind of power, she realized, like the rainspeakers had, and she shivered to think someday she might hold it herself.

She felt someone sit down next to her on her right, bringing a faint scent of wood-smoke and spice. As the story ended, she glanced over without moving her head. It was the young male from the drummers. He was cutting into an odd orange fruit covered with spiky horns, one she'd avoided at the feast because she wasn't sure how to eat it. As she watched furtively, he used a stone knife to cut the fruit in half across the shorter side, took up one of the halves with the cut side up, and squeezed it gently from the bottom. Pale green pulp bubbled up, and he put the half to his mouth and sucked it in.

He spat a few seeds to one side, then offered her the other half of the melon. "Want some? It's the last one. Won't get any more for a long time now."

So much for watching him furtively. Leya took the fruit and held it like he did. "What is it?"

"Kiwano. Your village doesn't get it? Your old village, I mean."

She shook her head. "Never seen it. It looked dangerous."

He chuckled. "Well, some things look that way until you know what to do with them. I mean, you look kind of dangerous yourself."

Her ears burned again. "I don't even have a spear yet."

"You look like you'd know what to do with it if you did," he said, an admiring note in his voice.

She tried the kiwano pulp, spitting out the seeds the way he did, though that made her even more self-conscious. It had a light, clean flavor, not as sweet as she'd expected.

The young male held out his hand, palm up. "I'm Nuru."

"Leya." Her hand was sticky, and she rubbed it on the

grass before brushing her fingers over his. The sensation tingled up her arm. She tried to ignore it.

"Do these grow here?" she asked.

"No. The sand-walkers bring them to trade; they only grow out there."

"Sand-walkers?"

"Jackals, mostly."

Leya fell silent again. There was so much she still hadn't seen, didn't know. She hoped he wouldn't ask where she'd been, hoped he didn't think she was stupid for not knowing more about the world past her own village. Then she wondered why she cared so much, already, about what he thought.

Beyond them, the great fire was dying down, and the night was quieting into softer conversations as the cubs were herded off to bed and others left the circle. Nuru stretched out beside her, hands behind his head, as simply as if they'd known each other forever. His mane, she noticed, went halfway down his toned chest, thinning to a dark point. He closed his eyes, and she used the chance to study his face. It was thinner than Bahati's, with a sharper muzzle and jaw. And he had a bit of kiwano pulp clinging to the corner of his mouth.

She wondered what he would do if she leaned in and licked it away. She'd never dare it, but her heart raced at the thought anyway. Bahati would have chuckled and called her his mother. What would Nuru do? What was such an insane thought doing in her head, anyway? And most importantly of all, was she always going to compare every male she saw to Bahati?

"You know," he said, eyes still closed, "it's hard to relax when you're thinking so loud."

She jumped. "What?"

He opened his eyes, gazed lazily up at her, his red-brown eyes like the shine on polished wood. "You just seem like you have too much on your mind for a night that's supposed to be a celebration."

"And how can you tell?" She was teasing him now, the way she would have teased Bahati. It was not what she would have done with any other male in her village.

But this wasn't Lwazi. And the Leya who'd lived there was dead, and her mother in mourning. She was Leya the *nakaranja* now. And who was anyone—even she herself—to say what Leya the *nakaranja* might do? Bold things, daring things, blood and fire and storm.

"Just a hunch," he said, smiling again, and she felt something in her rise to the surface, the way the pulp of the kiwano had burst through the cut surface.

She leaned down to him and licked the pulp from the corner of his mouth.

He gave a short, low-pitched growl, not surprise but pleasure, and licked her chin. He smelled of spice and the fruit and something else she couldn't identify, something warm and rich.

"Let's go for a walk," he said, and she agreed.

The earth beneath them had already cooled from the heat of the day, but Nuru's body was warm against hers as they lay amid the long grass just outside the village. She gazed up at the sky. They were the same stars as back home, the same as the ones she'd seen from one camp and another as the *karanja* followed the herds. Still, they looked different here. Or she felt different, and that was enough.

Nuru licked her ear, working his way back to her mouth. Slowly she groomed him in return, breathing in his scent. Since he'd led her here, they'd sometimes done this and sometimes talked, although she was finding she liked this just as well as talking. Perhaps more.

He pressed against her, his hands light over her fur. Once he moved a hand slowly up her thigh, but when she stiffened, uncertain, he moved away and went back to stroking her breasts. She relaxed again, glad he'd understood, because he was handsome and his mouth was sweet and his scent was making her dizzy and she really, really didn't want to have to kill him.

At last he groaned softly and moved away, adjusting his loincloth seemingly when he thought she wasn't looking. A new kind of pride rose in her. She had done that to him, just as he, though he couldn't see it so easily, had done the same to her. She wanted more but at the same time held back, as if she were approaching the wildebeest again, awed by their size and power, aware of a certain danger, aware she wasn't yet up to that hunt.

"So how much meat did you bring?"

The question startled her. "A zebra fresh. Four baskets of dried. Why?"

He chuckled. "Because I hope it runs out soon, and you can come back."

She lay her head on his chest. He stroked her breasts idly, lingering. "Shame to give these up," he murmured. "You're beautiful, Leya."

"Sometimes you have to make sacrifices."

"I know."

There was something in his voice that put more weight in the statement than she expected. Weight and a touch of sharpness. She glanced at him, curious, but unsure what to ask.

He shrugged. "Let's just say I know a lot about the *karanja*."

The knowledge didn't sound like it pleased him, and she bit back a sudden irritation, ready to defend her new sisters.

"How?"

He looked away, and his voice dropped low. "My mother was a *karanja*."

She sat up, staring at him. "Your... Your *mother*? But how..."

He shrugged, and she saw that easy light come back into his eyes. "Accidents happen sometimes. Like me."

She hesitated. "Where is she?"

"Gone now. A hunt went bad, or that's what I heard. She'd left me in her village, with her aunt, to raise me. I only saw her a few times after that. When they came to bring the meat." He shrugged again, as if it didn't matter, but she saw something different in his eyes.

"I'm sorry."

"It's not your fault."

"No, I mean... I'm sorry it had to be that way."

"It's like you said. Sacrifices. She made her choice. Anyway, it was a long time ago." He nuzzled her throat, her breasts. "Might as well enjoy these while they're there..."

While she still has them. The mocking voices of the village girls. And thoughts of Bahati again. The new Leya disappeared, clearing away like mist. His warmth against her still felt good, but she worried it was asking more than she should give.

She licked his muzzle again, slowly. "Nuru..."

"Mmm?"

"I... should probably get back to the tents. It's getting late." She tried to keep her voice light and soft, not wanting him to think she was refusing him entirely. It was as new and strange a skill, she thought, as learning to check the direction of the wind or how to predict where a spear would fly.

"All right. But—you *will* come back?"

"Of course."

"I don't just mean with the others. Not just to the village."

She smiled. "I know what you mean." She stood, breathed slow and deep, tasting the air, his scent, one last time, drawing it in, drawing it out. "Will you have more kiwano? I liked the way it tasted."

He chuckled as he led her back to the village. "If I have to go all the way to the sands myself, I'll find some for you. I promise."

回 ⚙ 回

Afternoon sun slanted on the red ochre tents. Beyond them, Thembe sighted along the length of Leya's spear, grunted softly, then held the spear point-down and dropped it onto a tsamma melon. The green rind split open. She nodded, drew the spear out, and then turned and threw it hard at the nearest thorn-tree. It stuck there in the trunk, quivering slightly.

At last Thembe brought the spear back to Leya. "Good."

Relief flooded her. This was the fourth spear she'd made; the others had cracked or broken outright at the last test.

"Give me your hand. Your throwing hand."

Leya held out her right hand. Thembe gripped her wrist firmly, turned her hand palm up, and drew the point across the pad, drawing a thin line of blood. Thembe wiped the spear-point across the blood, smearing it into each side. Then she held the spear in both hands and presented it to Leya. "Now it will fly true for you."

She'd already taught Leya why each *karanja* made her own weapons, that they carried part of the huntress' spirit with them, into the prey, to bring it down. Leya privately thought the huntresses had some... not *odd* feelings, exactly, about their weapons, but certainly intense ones. They weren't merely tools; they were part of each *karanja's* identity, and they were treated almost like children—or like gods. She didn't feel any of that for this spear, even after days of practice with it, but things might be different after a hunt.

As if hearing her thoughts, Thembe smiled. "There's no moon tonight, and the herds are close. A good night for a hunt."

Leya's heart leapt. "Tonight?"

"Are you ready?"

No. Leya swallowed, then lifted her chin. "Yes."

Thembe laughed. "Right now your zebra hide's cropping grass out there somewhere, *nakaranja*. Back to the tent now and rest, so you'll be ready to go and get it."

Leya went back to their tent, aware that this might be the last time she shared one with Thembe. After her kill, she'd have a tent of her own. She tried to sleep but dreamed of herds of zebra that turned and trampled her, so she spent the rest of the afternoon rubbing beeswax into the spear-shaft and gnawing on a strip of dried meat, eating enough to give her strength without slowing her down. She felt as if she should pray, but words wouldn't stay still long enough in her nervous mind to form any sort of prayer. Of anyone, she felt the Huntress would understand.

Night fell at last, and she met Thembe and Masika outside the tents. They would go with her to the herd but would stay at a distance, able to watch but not interfere. This was her hunt, her prey, her kill.

It was a small herd, mingled with gazelle and kudu. As she made her slow approach, she studied each zebra carefully, seeking out any weakness. To her dismay, they all looked strong, not to mention larger than she ever remembered zebra looking before.

Finally she settled on an older female, hoping age might slow the zebra down if nothing else. She moved closer, wanting to get to the edge of the long grass before she threw her spear.

A monkey called. Leya froze. A few of the antelope started, ears wide, listening, watching. A moment passed, and then they relaxed again. Another monkey answered the first.

Leya relaxed a bit herself. Not an alarm, then. She was still hidden. She waited a few moments more, counting breaths to ten, before she took another slow step forward. She was at the edge of the grass now; any farther and she might be seen. She kept her eyes locked on her target. The mare was by herself, a clear path for the spear.

She'd always imagined that she would be nervous at this point, but instead Leya felt a clear, deliberate calm she hadn't known was possible. There was no veld, no other world beyond this single creature, the pattern of its stripes, the weight of Leya's spear, her grip, her muscles, rising out of the crouch, the throw with her whole weight, her whole heart behind it, the singing rush of the spear through the air.

It struck the zebra at the base of the neck, and the creature bolted, sending the rest of the herd running. An instant later, the spear wobbled and dropped to the ground. The zebra ran on, only a trickle of blood to mark where she'd struck.

Leya stared at the scene, not sure whether to run after her spear or the zebra. Finally, when her muscles would listen again, she went for the spear, not wanting it to be trampled. By the time she reached it, the zebra were gone, and she stood in the crushing emptiness of the plain, all the weight of the night sky pressing down on her, listening to receding hoofbeats as if they were her heart.

Thembe. Masika. They were still out there. They had watched all of it.

She couldn't bear their rebuke, couldn't bear to think of their sympathy. Without any thought of where she was going, only away, Leya turned and ran.

"Leya?"

Bahati stood outside his hut, staring at her as if she were a spirit. She felt like one. She hadn't even known she was coming here, but here she was. And once she'd neared the village, she knew it wasn't home she wanted, wasn't her mother, wasn't her old life. It was him.

He shared a hut with two other young males, but thank Yaa, when she threw the stone at the hut, he was the one who came out.

"Leya," he said again, almost a whisper. "What's happened?"

She knew she'd been crying, though most of her journey from the herds to Lwazi was a dark blur. In reply, she jerked her head toward the veld, and he followed her out into the grass, out of the village and to the outcropping of rock where they'd lain the night before her initiation. There she told him everything, or as much of everything that mattered, the hunt at least, through tears and hitched breaths and her nose running into the fur of his chest as he held her.

"Shhh. It's okay."

"No, it's not."

"They give you another chance, don't they?"

"That's not the point." She scrubbed at her nose with the back of her hand. Already she felt like an idiot. Of course they'd give her another chance. What was she doing, crying like a cub, running to him now when she'd as good as told him she never wanted to see him again? And he hadn't even said anything about that, just acted like she'd never said it, never left, like everything was the same between them as it had always been.

"I'm sorry," he said softly, resting his chin on her head as they lay together against the rock. She wasn't sure exactly what he was apologizing for, but somehow everything from that night was slowly fading like mist.

"I'm sorry, too," she whispered. "I didn't mean…"

"I know."

And he did. And she knew he did, and something in that felt so completely right that the tears nearly started again. She snuggled closer. Yes, this was home, more than the village, more than the red tents, as much as her own body was home. And she knew, just as surely, that Bahati had no one else. If he had, he could never look at her the way he did, hold her the way he did.

She wasn't sure if she was the old Leya now or the new one. The new one liked the touch of Nuru's tongue, the danger and excitement of it, but only the old one, the one Bahati knew, could feel this quiet and safe, like the bird that was her soul had stopped beating its wings against the net and simply waited for what might come next.

"Bahati?" She loved the shape of his name in her mouth, the taste of it.

"Hm?"

"Bahati." Softly. Savoring the sound and the sureness of it.

He looked at her. Smiled that gentle smile.

"I love you," she said.

There was nothing else to say after that, nothing else that needed to be said. Touch was as good as words, and then better. She had felt excitement with Nuru; now she knew trust and love and the passion they woke within her. When his hand touched her thigh, she opened to him, and drew him down to her.

Once. Only once. But it was enough.

回 ⚙ 回

Leya woke first, just before sunrise. Bahati was snoring quietly beside her, his face in sleep looking like the cub's she remembered. She felt as if she were filled with sunlight, as if the vast sky itself could never hold everything she was feeling. She'd been a foolish cub for so long, so blind, so stubborn—but oh, she was wiser now. With his strength and belief behind her own, she could face anything. Even Masika.

Bahati lay with one arm outstretched, and Leya saw a bracelet on his wrist, beads separated by twine knots. The one he'd given her, the one she'd given back to him in anger. Had he worn it all this time? Gently, she bent her head to the inside of his wrist and brushed her muzzle over it.

"I love you," she whispered again, just for the pleasure of saying it out loud.

The sun glowed at the horizon. Leya stood and set out at a steady, loping pace, prepared to make a wide circle around the village, hoping she could get back to camp without being seen.

Then she saw the red tent—only one—set up just beyond the mud huts. A moment later, she heard voices she recognized.

Leya dropped into the tall grass, hoping it would hide her. There were only two *karanja* who would have come after her, and it wasn't Thembe's voice she heard.

"I thought she might have come here," Masika said. Leya had never heard the *karanjala* sound this way, softer, gentler, like any regular lioness instead of the commanding leader she'd always heard.

"If she did, she didn't come to me." Leya's mother.

Leya peeked slowly over the tips of the grass. The two lionesses sat on a fallen log, near enough for Leya to hear them, but, she hoped, far enough away that they wouldn't see or hear her. Masika, Leya noted, wasn't wearing her head-dress or her jewelry, and if it hadn't been for the *karanjala's* scars, it would have been difficult to tell the two women apart.

"I should have told her how many fail the first hunt," Masika said. "She hates to make mistakes. She takes so much to heart. And I forget that."

"Of course you forget," Naimah said, but her tone was light. "You were never that way. The more mistakes, the bet-ter—you always plowed on through. But Leya puts her heart into everything. When she was young, she scolded herself more for her mistakes than I ever did." Naimah paused as if deciding whether to go on. "She takes after her father, I think."

"Speaking of mistakes." There was a growl under Masika's words.

"Don't start, Sika." Naimah's voice was still light, but there was a warning note beneath.

It was like watching Bahati carve, like watching a blank piece of wood slowly become the shape of something else, something she recognized.

Sisters.

Of course they looked alike. All of a sudden she under-stood why her mother had been so worried about having ev-erything right when the *karanja* came.

Masika sighed and stood. "We'll hold camp for a few days. If you see her, tell her we're still there. Tell her there's no shame in it. As I should have."

"It's not your fault she's headstrong."

"No." Masika smiled, though her eyes glistened. "But I promised my sister I would look after her child. And I will." She rested a hand on Naimah's shoulder, then turned and walked back toward the tent.

◻ ⚙ ◻

The moon was a whisker of white light in the vast star-lit sky. Leya breathed in, breathed out, moved forward, and eyed the moonlight-edged herd. There, near the back—a female with the faintest of limps in her right hind leg. Perhaps a stone in the hoof.

Leya gripped her spear.

When she'd returned to camp, she'd found Masika and Thembe sitting outside the tents, as if waiting for her. They rose, but Leya spoke first.

"When can I try again?"

Kamara, Huntress, look kindly on your younger sister.

The zebra cropped another mouthful of dry grass. Leya listened to it chewing and took another slow, silent step closer.

Guide my spear to the center of the center.

She had spent the next days lifting stones, carrying water, throwing the spear farther, faster. She was stronger now. She could feel it.

Send it swiftly, send it sharply, O Huntress, my sister.

She was at the edge of the scrub now. She watched the zebra's sides bellow with each breath. The night was alive around her, within her. She breathed when the zebra breathed. She could almost taste the grass in its mouth, could almost feel hooves against the solid earth.

Guide my prey's spirit to the next world.

She drew her arm back, slowly, slowly, tensed, waiting for a signal in her breath, in her blood.

Not yet. Not yet.

Now.

Make its body strength for me and mine.

The spear sang a single note and then sank deep.

The herds moved away in a wave. Leya stood still and

watched. Her zebra tried to run, staggered, wheezed, stood panting.

She waited.

It took a few more jerking steps, its eyes rimmed with white. Then its front legs crumpled, as if it were lying down, but finally it fell on its side.

Leya moved out of the grass, hand to her knife. The spears brought them down but rarely killed them outright. But it was best that way, Thembe said. They were meant to look into the eyes of what they killed. It kept away the blood-madness, kept them from taking more than what they needed simply because they could.

Leya approached the zebra from its back, keeping clear of its hooves. Even a weak kick as it died could break ribs—or worse.

Its eyes were already beginning to glaze. Leya found the spot she'd been told to look for, knelt, and drew her knife across. Somewhere amid the scent of blood, the heat of it on her hands, she realized she was sobbing, and then it became laughter, both of them coming from someplace deeper in her than she knew she had.

Masika was there now; Thembe was there now. She was so weak they had to help her stand. Masika drew a knife and began slicing away the hide. Thembe cut the belly, drew out the liver, cut a piece from it, held it out to Leya.

"The rainspeaker," Leya said. "Its spirit—"

"This one," Thembe said, "you want in you. This is the price you pay."

Thembe put the bit of liver in Leya's mouth, soft and wet and mildly sweet. Leya swallowed it almost without chewing. She imagined the zebra's spirit in her stomach, in her blood, in her skin and fur, imagined seeing the world through its eyes.

Masika took the bloody hide and wrapped it around

Leya's hips to be sure there was enough. Leya swayed on her feet. Somewhere in the back of her mind, she saw a girl-cub with a sharpened stick, the cub she had been, and looked through her eyes again, and saw herself, and couldn't believe it, couldn't believe any of it.

Masika embraced her, and then Thembe was there. Leya fell to her knees, and they held her, and as her senses slowly returned, as she came back to herself again, she heard Masika's voice, strong and proud.

"*Karanja.*"

You won't feel it, Thembe told her.

Drink this.

There won't be pain.

Chew this, but don't swallow the leaves. Good.

Kamara will guide you through the feverlands. Follow her.

Close your eyes. Everything's fine.

Do you feel anything?

Now?

Kamara will guide you, Leya.

It's all right.

Just sleep now.

Everything's fine.

Kamara, we ask your protection…

Huntress, guide your sister…

Kamara looked young, no older than Leya herself, with a pale gold coat the same color of the dry grass that surrounded them. The Huntress wore strand after strand of bridal necklaces, and when Leya looked down she realized she was holding a strand of her own, every bead glistening with her own red blood. Leya slipped it over Kamara's head and embraced her. Kamara's claws dug deep into Leya's back, and the Huntress' jaws closed at the base of Leya's throat, and she couldn't breathe, couldn't see, couldn't feel anything.

They were cutting her open. She heard Thembe's voice, Masika's, the rainspeaker's. They cut out her heart and passed it from one to the next, chewing the tough meat, their muzzles stained red. They cut open her lungs, and all the words she had ever spoken flew out and buzzed around them like a swarm of bees, and flew away. They cut open her belly and lifted out vipers, one after the other, hissing and striking, and draped them around each other's necks.

She stood on an endless plain. Kamara was there again, but this time with full, heavy breasts and a gently rounded belly. "Who's the father?" Leya asked, but the Huntress only laughed, a high, mocking giggle like the spiteful girls in the village.

"*You* know," the Huntress said, "and I have him, and you don't. He'll never look at you again."

She was on fire, burning down to her bones, and the bones blew away like dust.

She was swimming through mud.

She was holding half a kiwano, squeezing the bottom to bring up the pulp, only it wasn't a melon; it was her mother's heart, and it was sweet, and the juice ran down her chin.

She was nursing a cub, but when it pulled away from her breast, it had no face, only the rounded stump of a muzzle and a blank expanse of fur.

She was flying into a blue sky, higher and higher, seeing and smelling and tasting nothing but sky, blue and cool, so pure it burned.

An elephant calf lay trapped under a net of bridal twine. Its skin was white, not merely pale but white, and it glowed, and its skin was so thin that every blood vessel stood out like the branches of a tree silhouetted against the sky.

Her knife was in her hand.

"Free it," Kamara said. She looked like Masika now.

"I can't. It'll destroy everything."

"Free it."

And Leya cut into the translucent hide, and it parted like water at the touch of the blade, and broke open, and light spilled out, golden light like a hundred sunrises, flooding out over her, washing over her.

Somewhere a cub cried out and then fell silent.

Slowly Leya felt the weight of her own limbs, the net of skin and fur that held her together, the rhythm of her breath, the drum of her heart, the solid earth beneath her body. Slowly she understood that she was Leya, not a spirit, not the elephant calf. She remembered who Leya was, and that it was her.

Slowly she opened her eyes.

Chapter 3

As the huts of Lwazi finally came into view, Leya fought the urge to start running. As it was, she walked just a little faster while still keeping a solid grip on the front end of the kudu carcass she was carrying, and Thembe, who had shouldered the back end, had to jog a bit to keep up. Leya glanced back, ready to apologize, but the white lioness just smiled. *She remembers how it was*, Leya thought, and smiled herself.

The wounds on her chest had nearly healed. The long thorns that had held her skin together in some places were long since removed, and the neat lines of gut stitches were being absorbed back into her body. The skin there was still bare, but by the time her fur had grown back in, the scars would be almost invisible. It didn't look like her body, and yet it looked the way she'd always dreamed it would.

She had spent twelve days in the feverlands, as Thembe told her later. It seemed impossible that it could have been so long, and yet equally impossible that it could have been so short.

"There's no time in the feverlands," Thembe had said with a shrug. "But sometimes we weren't sure if Kamara was leading you back to this world or on to the next."

For the first few days, she didn't remember anything from that time, but bit by bit, flashes of memory and images, swift as lightning-strikes and as stunning, came back to her as she healed. She wanted to ask Thembe about them, or maybe Zhenga the rainspeaker, but the white lioness stopped her sharply. "What you saw there was only for you. You shouldn't talk about it to anyone else, and never ask anyone else what they saw."

Leya nodded, though she was disappointed she wouldn't get help unraveling the knotted strands of images. The elephant calf, especially, came back in her dreams, sometimes several nights in a row, then staying away for several more, wandering the landscape of her mind. Sometimes the calf glowed like it had in the feverlands, its veins pulsing with golden light, and other times it looked normal, with a gray-brown hide smeared with mud against the sun and the flies. It never spoke, but there was a sharp focus to its eyes that made Leya think it could. In the dreams, she often tried to speak to it, but every time she found that she'd forgotten the sounds that made words.

During her waking hours, though, she was happy, and more satisfied with the world than she thought she could ever feel. She'd killed two of the gazelles that made up the dried meat they were taking to the village, and she loved knowing that her own people would be eating what she'd killed, that her hunt would keep them well and strong. Secretly she'd set aside a handful of particularly nice morsels for Bahati, packing them with her own rations. She imagined putting the bits on his tongue, telling him about the hunt while he ate. The thought sent a shivering heat through her. Now that she had a tent to herself, she had spent many nights lying in the darkness thinking of him, touching where he had touched until her breath hitched and her muscles clenched. But it was never the same as his touch, never his scent or his weight on her, his voice or his love, and that was what she longed for.

And now, at last, she would see him again. She wondered if he would be there to meet them, or if he would wait until the fire-circle after dark. She spent the rest of the walk trying to think of something clever to say to him when she first saw him, but she was too restless and excited to think of anything good.

The *aumah* was waiting for them, and Masika presented him with the meat. The village rainspeaker said the usual prayer. Leya sneaked glances around the village. Most of the women were carrying pots and baskets of food to the fire-circle. Cubs chased each other around the huts, playing a game Leya remembered. Three older males played a game of chance with stones and beads in the shade of one of the huts. She didn't see Bahati. She was just about to go look for him when Masika placed a hand on her shoulder.

"Your mother will want to see you," Masika said.

Leya nodded, though she couldn't help looking in the direction of Bahati's hut. She found the path to her mother's hut without having to think, as if she had just been out on the veld practicing her tracking with Bahati and was coming home for a meal.

The air, the earth, the scents of cooking-fires—all of it smelled the same. Nothing about the village itself looked different, but everything felt different. Amid these huts, she was a cub again, and all the good and bad memories of those years swarmed around her.

The gray-white fur at her mother's nose and mouth surprised her, and then she scolded herself for being surprised. There was no reason why she could expect her mother, of all the world, to be spared by time.

"Leya." Naimah brought her arms up as if to embrace her, but then the lioness' gaze went to Leya's chest. Naimah held her arms across her own, almost hugging herself. Leya couldn't tell what she might be thinking.

"Mother." She wasn't sure what she was going to say next; all she wanted was to bring her mother's gaze back to hers, away from what she had lost, so Naimah could see what she'd gained, what she'd become.

"You look… well," Leya offered.

It wasn't the truth. Naimah looked tired, and Leya wondered how long she had been up the night before, cooking and preparing as she always had.

"So do you," Naimah said, but she could tell that was only being polite as well.

Leya searched for some safe topic. "How's Ayanna?"

"She had her cubs, six days ago. Twin boys. They're beautiful. You should see them."

Leya flinched back from the praise. *You should see them,* she heard. *See what you could have had.* As if it would make any difference. As if it would have made any difference even before. She'd played with spears and slingshots as a cub, never the dolls the other girl-cubs had so fastidiously mothered.

She wanted to tell her mother she was happy. She wanted to tell her mother she loved Bahati, that he loved her. She wanted to tell her mother about the zebra hide she wore now, about the necklace with its bone and tooth and ivory beads, and what it all meant. She wanted to share all of it, wanted Naimah to understand.

But she wouldn't. Mention Bahati and there would be false hope, or anger at lost opportunity. Mention the hunt, and there would be polite interest but no enthusiasm.

She realized she wanted her mother to see her as a woman, but she didn't. Before, Leya had been a cub. Now her mother kept looking at her as if she were—not male, but yet something not quite female either. Not a woman, but more like a spear or a knife given a person's shape.

All she saw, Leya realized, was what wasn't there. All she saw were the paths Leya couldn't walk, and not the ones she could.

"I should go see Ayanna before it gets dark," Leya said finally. The tightness of her chest, the tightness of her smile were getting too much to bear.

Her mother handed her a small covered basket that was warm and smelled of honey. "I made you some safou cakes." Naimah looked uncertain. "If you still like them."

"I do." Leya found herself smiling at the familiar scent. "They had them in the other villages sometimes, but they were never as good."

Her mother nodded.

Leya looked at her mother's tired face, imagined her working honey into the dough, making small round cakes, pressing the fruit in and tucking the dough around it, all the time her mother's hands working with swift, sure, gentle movements. For her. As they always had. She smiled again, and this time it was real. "Thank you."

Her mother nodded again. "It'll be dark soon."

"Will you be at the circle tonight?"

Her mother hesitated. "I'll see," she said, which they both knew meant no.

Leya gripped the basket against her belly, holding on to the warmth. She wasn't sure whether to say good-bye, but finally she just nodded and left. She found herself sighing deeply as she walked away, as if she'd been carrying a full calabash and finally set it down.

She looked for Bahati again but didn't see him. Of course—he'd be waiting for her in the veld, at the kopje just outside the village. That was the best place anyway, away from any chance the *karanja* might guess there was more between them than simply a night's pleasure.

"Leya!" Ayanna called to her from the doorway of her hut. Leya sighed a little at the delay but went over.

Ayanna looked much the same as she had on her wedding night, though now the strands of bridal beads had been replaced by a sling that held two newborn cubs close to her chest.

"We're thinking of calling them Asabi and Abasi," Ayanna said. "Aren't they beautiful?"

Leya held her tongue on the wisdom of giving them such similar names. Knowing Ayanna, she might change her mind a dozen times before the naming ceremony, always held at the third full moon after a cub's birth, when its spirit entered its body.

"They're so tiny," Leya said at last, and though it seemed a stupidly obvious thing to say, Ayanna beamed as if it were a compliment.

"They should be. They're only six days old." Ayanna chuckled. "I've spent the past six days just counting fingers and toes. Over and over. Isn't that silly?"

"Mm." Was she supposed to agree with that, or disagree? All of a sudden Leya felt like she was back stringing beads again, all the wrong ones in a row.

Still… She tried to grasp the feeling that came with looking at the twins. Six days ago these cubs—these people—hadn't been here. And now they were. New, and different from anyone who had ever been here before, or ever would be. How strange, and how wonderful.

She thought about telling Ayanna this, but she couldn't find the right words and was afraid of being misunderstood. Their paths had taken them such different places. Leya felt happy for her, but being happy wasn't the same as understanding, as *knowing*.

Every woman in this village, Leya realized, understood Ayanna's joy. But not one of them would know what it meant to watch that zebra crumple to the ground, to hold a knife and cut its throat because it meant everything you'd ever wanted. She could tell Ayanna about it, and her friend would smile and nod in the right places, but that would be all.

She'd been silent too long; she could feel it. "They're beautiful, Ayanna." Yaa's whiskers, what else did people say?

Ayanna's eyes lit up. "Do you want to hold them?"

Leya gestured with the basket in both hands. "Oh, I'd… I'd better get to the fire. They're waiting for me. It was good to see you."

Ayanna nodded. One of the cubs gave a short cry and diverted her attention, and Leya used the moment to slip away. Leaving the basket by the fire-circle, she picked up the old trail and followed it into the veld.

She quickened her pace to match her heart, walking, then running. She remembered the feeling of flying in the feverlands, into that dizzying blue sky. That was what she felt now, only keener, sharper. As she approached the kopje, she squinted at its silhouette, trying to find his shape among the rocks. But likely he was sitting in front of it, as they often did.

She could tell him everything. He would understand. He would know.

And then, later, when the moon edged the grass with light…

She reached the rocks, heart pounding, and circled around them to the front.

He wasn't there.

She checked the position of the sun. Still a while before they'd be lighting the fire and she'd be expected there.

She climbed to the top, watched the wind through the grass, and waited. Every rustle in the veld, every hint of movement made her tense and look around expectantly. Once she thought she caught his scent faint on the wind, but nothing else happened.

Someone was coming. Leya's pulse raced again, and then a male voice spoke beside her. Not his.

"Leya?"

She turned. It was Miombo, one of the males Bahati shared a hut with. Was Bahati sick? Had something happened?

"Where's Bahati?" she asked. She heard fear in her voice and tried to tone it down. "I've been looking for him. Have you seen him?"

Miombo looked out into the veld. She watched his tongue test the point of one tooth. "He's not here anymore."

"What?"

"He left. Just after the long rains."

Leya stared at him. "Left? Where?"

"I don't know." Miombo shrugged helplessly. "He didn't talk to us about it. He didn't talk to anybody about it. He came out here a lot. And then he told us he was leaving, and he told the *aumah*, and…" Miombo shrugged again.

There were no words. There was no breath. She couldn't stop staring at him, waiting for him to say something else, to say he was wrong. To say that Bahati was waiting for her somewhere else, somewhere she hadn't thought to look.

"So. Anyway." Miombo ran a hand through his mane. "He told me to give this to you, if I saw you."

He held it out, and she took it. Her bracelet. She closed her fingers around it. The beads felt cool at first on the pad of her palm, then warmed. One bead for lots of zebra. One for not getting stung by bees. One for happiness.

Miombo had gone. That was good. She had almost thanked him, out of habit, and how could she thank anyone for this?

She sat on the rock, waiting to feel something, like watching clouds gather for rain. In her mind, she pictured herself biting the knots between the beads, throwing each one into the veld, as far as she could, with her teeth clenched and her chest tight.

But the old anger wouldn't come, and she felt as abandoned by it as she did by Bahati.

The sun was setting, and darkness would come fast. Leya looked down at the bracelet. She wanted to put it on. She wanted to never see it again. She hated Bahati, loved him, each one as fierce as the other.

Finally she wedged the bracelet into a crevice in the rock where they'd hidden things as cubs. It was a cub's romance anyway, she told herself. She could have someone in every village if she wanted. That was how the *karanja* lived, and she was *karanja* now.

They would be lighting the fire already. Leya forced

down something hot and desperate within herself, as deep as it would go, and found the trail back to the village. There was nothing here for her anymore, not in the veld, not in her mother's hut, not in her mother's eyes. She knew she would have to come back sometimes, but she vowed to go no farther than the fire-circle. That was the only place in a village that any *karanja* belonged.

◙ ۞ ◙

Rains came, passed, came again. In every village, she still looked for him, though every time she swore she wouldn't. It didn't matter; he was never there.

In the height of the lush wet season, they went to the village of Thutiwa again. She was searching the villagers for Bahati when she caught a flash of something orange in the corner of her vision. She turned just in time to catch it, her body reacting before her mind could, and a kiwano's blunt spikes dug into her hands.

She looked up to see Nuru's red-brown eyes as he grinned at her. "Saved it for you," he said.

The weight of the fruit felt good in her hands. She remembered the taste of it lingering in his mouth. Something flickered within her. "What else have you saved for me?"

His smile broadened. "Take a walk with me, *karanja*, and I'll show you."

◙ ۞ ◙

There were advantages, Leya thought later that night, to having a lover who knew the *karanja*'s ways as well as Nuru did. He already knew the once-a-night limit without being told—not to mention a number of other ways to pleasure them both that didn't count toward it. She was grateful for the easy exhaustion that filled her now, that helped her forget the rest of the world beyond this patch of tall grass, the rest of her life except for these moments.

She watched him sleep, his lean body carved by the moonlight. He hadn't hesitated at the scars on her chest, hadn't looked at her the way the others in her village did now, as if she were no longer a woman and yet not a man. He'd only traced the scars with his fingertips, neither lingering over them nor shying away from them. She'd relaxed fully then, and the rest of the evening was a pleasant haze.

The *karanja* would move on, as they always did, and Nuru would stay. When she returned, he would be waiting. What either of them did in between was of no concern. He would never ask more of her than she could give.

That was the way it should be, she thought as she fell asleep. Nuru was handsome, he made her laugh, he excited her with the most casual touch. What more did she need?

She woke just past sunrise and stretched the hard ground from her limbs. Nuru stirred beside her and gave her a languid smile.

"So who's Bahati?" he asked.

"Bahati." She tried to say the name as if she'd never heard it before.

"You said it a few times in your sleep. Figured it was somebody's name." He nuzzled her neck. "Another conquest of yours?"

"No." She buried her nose in his mane, breathing spice, and pressed her body against his. "Nobody I know. You shouldn't pay any attention to the nonsense I say in my sleep."

"What about the nonsense you say when you're awake?"

She growled softly and nipped his ear. This was all she needed, she told herself. The playful game, the desire, the release. Nothing more to think of, nothing more to feel.

Really, she told herself, it was better this way.

◨ ⚙ ◧

The veld dried from green to blond, and the clear blue sky burned. Leya crouched in the dry riverbed, dug up a handful of earth, and watched the dust sift through her fingers. She would never have believed a river could disappear, but it had. That morning, Masika had gazed into a sky that should have been heavy with rain. They would break camp the day after tomorrow, the *karanjala* declared, unless rain came. Otherwise they risked too much of their prey moving on without them.

Every day they walked farther for water. Every day they watched the earth crack and buckle. Leya knew there had been a time when the veld was green, a time when her mouth didn't taste of grit, but it seemed more like a dream now than a memory. The moon had waxed and waned twice since they'd been to any of the villages, not wanting to be a burden on the villagers' limited water. The *karanja* looked after themselves.

Leya squinted into the distance, looking across the veld. She could just make out the form that she knew was Zhenga, their rainspeaker, sitting out in the open sun, though there was shade from a thorn-tree not three steps away. She had been there two days and two nights without moving. Leya hoped she was still alive.

Well, she was a rainspeaker; she knew what she was doing. Leya picked up the empty calabash and walked on to the water hole.

She felt them before she saw them. It was a vibration in her breastbone, as if the dry packed earth had been struck like a drum. Gray shapes shimmered at the horizon.

Elephants.

Leya felt a sudden strange anticipation, as if the rains had been given a creature's shape. They were only coming to drink, she knew; this was the last water in at least half a day's walk. And yet she stared at the horizon as they drew closer, as if they came for her.

What would it be like to see the world from that height, to carry such power within you and know it was there with every step?

The feverlands calf flashed into her mind and was gone. Leya shook herself a bit, filled the calabash, and headed back to the tents. There was no message in their coming, she told herself. They needed water like everything else.

Back at the tents, the *karanja* looked as they had when Leya had been an initiate. Everyone lay sprawled on mats in the shade of open tents, no one moving more than she had to in the heat. Leya took Thembe a gourd of water, and the white lioness tilted it a bit, as if to spill it on the ground, then smiled and drank.

When the gourd was empty, Thembe sighed slow and deep. "I've been lying here so long my bones are turning into rock. We need a hunt."

"Too hot," Nanji grumbled from her tent.

"Too lazy," Thembe said. "It'll be cooler when the sun's gone, anyway. Come on. Easy prey out there now, and you know it."

Thembe nudged and prodded and insulted and threatened, and at last they agreed. "Good," she said aside to Leya. "When all there is to do is wait and worry about things, *karanja* start getting soft inside, like a melon rotting. Remember that. When you're worried, go hunt something."

The cooler air of twilight woke them up and stirred their blood. Leya thought they would go to the water hole and hunt there, but Thembe told her it was bad luck to kill something as it came to drink in the dry times, so bad that it might keep the rain from ever coming again.

"But Kamara killed the elephant at the water hole, didn't she?"

"The elephant gave herself," Thembe corrected her.

"But Kamara would have killed the calf, and that was at the water hole."

"And when you see her in the next world, you can ask her about it." Thembe glanced at their rainspeaker as they passed, still motionless on the veld. "Or you could ask Zhenga, but I think she dried up over there and if we touch her, she'll crumble."

They fell silent then as they neared the water, looking over the small groups of bony antelope and zebra, some more flies than hide. Thembe was right; it would be an easy hunt.

Nanji skirted around and moved in closer, checking positions, the wind, the straggling movement of their prey. The creatures were skittish and tense, their precious energy burning itself in nervous bursts.

At last Nanji signaled back to the others. Kudu, male, limp on the left hind. When Leya looked closer, she saw a thick swelling on that leg, buzzing with flies. Its horns were beautiful; they would make for good trade to a village *aumah*.

Her heart beat faster, as if it matched her prey's. Even now, after dozens of hunts, the sensation thrilled her. She never felt more alive than in this moment.

In Leya's line of sight, Masika took one more slow step to the edge of the scrub. For a moment, Leya saw Kamara as she must have looked, in the long time before, drawing back her arm, muscles tensed, letting the spear fly.

The veld went silent but for Leya's heartbeat.

Masika's spear struck home, and the world exploded into sound again, the kudu snorting and breaking into a run. The spear-point hadn't gone deep, though, and the shaft bobbed and jerked as the creature ran. Leya ran along the kudu's path, trying to predict where it would be, how it might turn, waiting for the right moment.

The kudu shook off Masika's spear, and Leya paused,

steadied herself quickly, and threw hers. Panicked, the creature bucked and bolted in a new direction.

Straight toward Thembe.

Instinctively Thembe started to raise her spear, but the kudu was already on top of her. In a slow, nightmarish blur, Leya saw the lioness fall, saw the kudu scramble over her, one hoof opening a gash, another striking her hard in the ribs. It all happened in the space of a heartbeat.

Leya ran to Thembe. The white lioness had her hands pressed against her belly, but her coat and the ground beneath were already bright red. The same color blood as their prey, Leya thought in a sudden daze, the same color they saw all the time, but somehow this seemed darker, brighter, more vivid.

Masika was there an instant later, stripping off her zebra hide and pressing it against the wound. "Back to camp," Masika said. "Leya, hold her head. Gently now."

Together Masika, Nanji, and Leya carried Thembe back to her tent and washed her wound with the muddy water. "Get Zhenga," Masika told Nanji.

"She's still out there praying. What if she won't come?"

"Drag her," Masika said through clenched teeth. "If Yaa hasn't gotten her message by now, he's not much of a god."

Leya sat by Thembe's head, wanting to do something but not sure what. The lioness' eyes were unfocused, and she was panting. Pain? Fear? Both? Leya took Thembe's hand between her own, both to comfort the lioness and try to slow her own racing heart.

Zhenga returned then. The rainspeaker's jaw set grimly as she surveyed the wound. Leya saw the look she exchanged with Masika, but the rainspeaker tended the wound as best she could, sewing the ragged edges back together. Then she pressed lightly into Thembe's side, and Thembe cried out, the sound loud and sharp in the tense silence. Leya flinched, feeling as if she'd been struck.

"Broken," Zhenga said.

"How many?" Masika asked.

"Two, maybe three."

"The gut?"

Zhenga spread her hands wide. "Yaa's hands. Not mine."

Leya wanted to ask what could be done, but her tongue stuck to the roof of her dry mouth, and she couldn't seem to work it free enough to speak. She didn't like Masika's expression, though, and she liked the rainspeaker's even less.

Zhenga left to prepare a tonic for the pain. Masika and Leya were alone with Thembe now, Leya still holding Thembe's hand.

"What do we do?" Leya whispered.

"Wait," Masika said. Her voice broke. "Pray."

Leya did more of both in the days that followed than she ever had in her life. She prayed to Yaa, to Kamara, to her own family's ancestors, and sometimes just to the sky, just a wordless, desperate pleading exhaled with every breath.

At last, late that evening, around the time they'd set out for the hunt the day before, Thembe woke with a groan. Leya was alone with her, though Masika had come in several times as the day wore on.

"Lie still," Leya said. "It's all right."

Thembe's eyes searched back and forth. "Camp?"

"We carried you back. It's all right now; just rest." She pressed a wet scrap of hide against Thembe's mouth, letting a few drops trickle in.

"Not as fast as I... used to be." Thembe tried to sit up but gasped hard with the pain and lay still again.

"Did you get him?" Thembe asked after a moment.

"Get who?"

"The kudu."

Leya shook her head.

Thembe swore softly. "Have to get him myself later, then. Like to eat that one's heart."

Masika came in then with a gourd of something that smelled mostly of honey but with something bitter underneath. "Is the pain bad?"

"Well, first I was afraid I was going to die, and now I'm afraid I'm not."

Masika managed a slight smile. "Drink this; it'll help."

Thembe drained the gourd, grimaced, and handed it back. "Tell the bees to work harder. It'll take more honey than that to cover up whatever that is."

"I'll give Zhenga your compliments," Masika said, and slipped out.

Thembe closed her eyes, and after a while Leya thought she'd fallen asleep. Then Thembe spoke. "Leya?"

"I'm here." Leya swallowed. "Thembe, I'm so sorry—I didn't know it was going to—"

"Don't mind that. Been hurt before, lots of times. They do what they do." Thembe sighed drowsily. "Maybe that honey stuff isn't so bad after all. Nice and warm..."

"I'll be right here," Leya said. "Just rest."

"Mm. Tell me a story, then. What's the last one you learned again?"

"Kamara and the termite queen."

"That's a good one. Tell me that one."

Leya's throat ached with the tears she was keeping back, but she managed to start anyway. Halfway through the story, Thembe's breathing grew deep and even. Leya kept going, one sentence following another, finding comfort in the rhythm, and finished the story in a whisper.

Day dragged after day. The rains still didn't come, and the only time Leya left Thembe's side was to walk to the water hole. It, too, was shrinking bit by bit, and she had to carefully navigate the dark, sticky mud to get to the part that was deep enough to fill the calabash. The rest of the time, Leya stayed in Thembe's tent, coaxing her to drink broth or water, helping her up enough to relieve herself, talking when Thembe wanted to talk, sitting silently by as she slept. The doses of Zhenga's tonic went down without further complaint, though Leya worried at how many she was taking. Still, she told herself the *karanja* had seen injury before. Hadn't they tended her safely through twelve days of fever?

One afternoon, as Leya returned with another gourd of water—skimmed from the surface in the calabash, to try to keep out the worst of the silt—Thembe stirred, half-asleep. "Kendi?"

Leya frowned at the unfamiliar name. "Thembe, it's me. Leya."

Thembe came fully awake then and caught Leya's expression. "What?"

"You called me Kendi."

"Oh." Thembe smiled, took a sip of the water, and lay carefully back down again. "Dreaming, I guess."

"Who is she?"

"Was," Thembe said softly. "My little girl. Beautiful little girl-cub."

Leya stared at her. Thembe had never mentioned having had a cub before, not in all sorts of different conversations. She wondered what other things remained hidden beneath the still water of Thembe's eyes, and she also wondered how many secrets she might carry herself by the time she was Thembe's age.

"How old was she? How old were you?"

"I was about your age, maybe a few rains older. She lived for a day and a night. Beautiful day. Beautiful night." Thembe took a wheezing breath and reached for the water again. "They told me not to name her, because she didn't have a spirit yet."

Leya nodded.

"But her eyes... She looked right at me. She knew me. She knew herself. I think she even knew she didn't have long. So I named her anyway. What did any of them know?"

Leya smiled at the defiance in her second mother's voice, weak as she was. "And... her father?"

"Left. Thought it was my fault, though he never said it. He didn't have to. And then I came here," Thembe finished, as if it had been that simple, though Leya knew it couldn't have been.

Thembe's gaze was distant, locked somewhere in the past. "Oh, I was angry. At him, at all the gods, at everything. This whole world and the next. Everything I ate tasted sour. I wanted to kill things. I wanted blood." She smiled at the memory the way a parent might smile at an unruly child, equal parts patience and exasperation and love.

"I didn't understand anything," Thembe went on. "All I knew was, I'd had everything I ever wanted, and then it was all gone. And I didn't know what else to want. Didn't know there was even anything else worth wanting."

Leya had no idea what to say.

"Sometimes you remind me of her," Thembe said. "When I first saw you—saw your eyes—they looked like hers. Like they wanted to drink up the whole sky, and know everything there was to know. I knew then I had to be the one to kindle you. Whatever it took."

Leya laughed. "It took a lot."

Thembe tried to laugh but wound up coughing, and

then her breath cut off in a gasp at the pain in her side. Leya brought more of the tonic, and Thembe swallowed it without protest.

"Tell me a story," Thembe said then, closing her eyes.

"Which one?"

"Tell me a story of Leya, the huntress, in her village."

Leya's entire past went blank in her mind. Finally she seized on the story about collecting ants for a trick the cubs had played on the vainest lioness in Lwazi.

Thembe listened, smiled, and drifted into sleep. Leya sat by her side for a long time, watching her breathe, trying to imagine Thembe at her age, trying to imagine being Thembe back then, being Thembe now.

It was like everyone carried a whole village inside them, she realized, all the people they used to be, all the people they were, all the people they might be. She wondered what the village inside her would look like, and whether she would even recognize all of her selves if she went there.

◙ ⚙ ◙

Every day, clouds built up in the afternoon. The air cooled, and Leya grew hopeful, watching the sky, but then the clouds dissipated, and the earth was still a hard-baked crust. She figured she had only a few more days before the water hole turned to nothing but mud. After that, she would have to walk farther, and hope more.

Thembe grew no better but no worse. Leya tried to take hope from the sameness, but something in Masika's eyes worried her. *She's seen this before,* Leya thought, *or something like it,* and she wanted to ask but didn't really want to know.

The next morning, she woke in Thembe's tent to find the pads of the lioness' hands and feet slick with sweat. Thembe's eyes were glassy. She called Leya by her daughter's name again, and spoke as if she lived in a village, as if the years had rolled back.

Leya ran for Masika and Zhenga. They took the coverings from Thembe's wound. The stitches held, but the flesh was red and swollen.

"Fever," Zhenga said, her voice flat.

Masika blew out a breath and turned away. "Yaa's cock," she muttered, "where are the damned rains?"

Leya heard her aunt draw in a breath and let it out again. When Masika turned back, she was the *karanjala* again, jaw set, head high. "Keep mud on her pads," she told Leya. "It'll cool her for a few moments, at least."

Leya nodded. There were other instructions, worried glances, and then she and Thembe were alone again.

The *karanja* had seen her through the feverlands. Now she had to do the same for Thembe. Was Kamara the Huntress there to guide her? Or was Thembe's daughter there, grown up and beautiful, ready to tempt her into the next world instead? She thought of her own visions there and shuddered.

The day might as well have been ten. Leya scooped cool mud from the bottom of the calabash and spread it over Thembe's pads, then took the long walk back to the water hole. A trio of baboons shrieked at her from the opposite side, and she threw a rock at them, scattering them, just to be able to throw something as hard as she could. She thought it might make her feel better, but it didn't.

She filled the calabash and lifted it to her head. On the way back, she saw Zhenga out on the veld again, this time dancing with slow, measured steps around a water-gourd. The rainspeaker wore a wooden mask of an elephant's head, and Leya caught the sound of a bone rattle. She looked away and went back to the tent.

The only advantage to the drought was that prey was easy to find. The larger herds had moved on, but Masika and the others easily brought down stragglers weakened by thirst and starvation. Leya tried to get Thembe to drink broth, but half the time she threw it back up not long after.

Just before dark that evening, Thembe woke as Leya came in with another dose of the tonic. Leya put the gourd to Thembe's mouth, but Thembe raised a hand clumsily to push it away.

"Not yet," Thembe said, her voice a rough whisper. She was having more trouble breathing, and the wound at her belly oozed pale green.

"I wanted to tell you," Thembe went on. "If you ever see him again, don't—be too hard on him."

"What? Who?"

"Your lover. The real one. I don't know his name."

"Bahati," Leya whispered. It was the first time she'd said it out loud since the day she'd found him gone.

Thembe nodded. "You know—men aren't given many more ways to be—than we are."

"Ways to be?"

"Like us. Girls, mothers, karanja, old. All those little boxes, like you had to put the ants in. Too small for us. Too small for the men, too."

Leya shook her head. "I don't understand."

"You will sometime." Thembe managed a smile. "Just hold on to it."

"He couldn't even tell me goodbye."

"Not every man—can be a karanja's lover. Maybe he couldn't. And maybe he knew it. Try to forgive him." Her eyes went distant, and Leya wondered if she was thinking of her own mate. "I never could," Thembe said.

"Did you ever see him again?"

Thembe shook her head slightly. "Could have looked for him, I guess. Too proud to do it. Too young to know—he was just hurting too—same as I was."

Leya wondered for the hundredth time if she would ever see Bahati again. She could look for him, too, more than she'd been doing, but she wasn't sure she wanted to. Was that pride, or was she just afraid of finding out for certain that she didn't matter to him anymore, would never matter to him again?

"I should have listened to you before," Leya said.

Thembe smiled slightly. "Which time was that?"

"You told me we give our bodies. Never our hearts."

"Mm." Thembe was silent for a long moment, then sighed. "That's the safe way. The easy way. If you have the choice." She sighed again. "But you don't always get a choice. You don't get to stop feeling something—the way you can stop running—and stand still. It has its own time. Like the rains."

Thembe fell silent again then, and after a few moments Leya realized she was asleep. The calabash of water was almost empty again; this would be a good time to take the long walk and fill it again while she slept.

The clouds were gathering again, but Leya took no hope from them. They would have been darker and heavier if they were carrying rain. Once the last of this water dried up, they'd have to move on, even though Thembe was in no shape to travel. They'd have to carry her somehow, maybe build a frame to carry her on…

She was trying to figure out how it would be best to make it when she saw the shape at the edge of the water. At first, she thought it was a rock, exposed as the water disappeared. Then she saw it move, just slightly, and realized it was something alive, something huddled there in the dark mud.

Leya had left her spear on the veld when Thembe had gotten hurt. She hadn't been back to look for it since. Still, she had her knife, so she gripped that just in case and went cautiously forward.

It was an elephant calf, lying on its side, partially submerged in the thick mud.

For an instant Leya saw the calf from the feverlands instead, the pale skin and the blood beneath. Then it was gone, just a gray elephant calf again, too exhausted to do anything but breathe.

And Kamara knew her sister was dying.

Thembe was dying. Masika wouldn't say it. The rainspeaker wouldn't say it. They didn't have to.

And so she went to the last place where water still stood.

Leya set the calabash down and moved slowly toward the calf. She could tell it knew she was there, but it didn't move, didn't make a sound. She looked at her own reflection in its dark eye fringed with soft lashes.

To find a spirit to give in place of her sister.

It had come to drink. She saw it as clearly as if she had watched it happen. It had gotten trapped in the mud, too small and weak to pull itself out. The adults would have tried to pull it free, tried to get trunks underneath it to lift it to its feet. At last, they moved on. There would be no mother here to give her life to save her calf's.

Leya reached out slowly and laid a hand on the calf's side, feeling the breath move through it, feeling the blood move through it, as if she could see every vessel.

I come with fear of death, for my sister, who is half my heart, lies dying, and I will have another's spirit to give Yaa in her stead.

So she might live.

She thought of the knife-blade in her vision, the flesh parting like water, the light pouring out.

It was going to die anyway, starvation and thirst, worse deaths than the quick cut of a blade. This was not a hunt; it was mercy, for the calf and for Thembe both.

She prayed for strength. At last she gripped the knife, crouched down by the calf, found the vein, and pushed the blade in. She had to hold the knife with both hands to make the full cut. Hot blood sprayed over her hands and settled like a skin over the surface of the mud.

Leya dropped to her knees in the mud and leaned against the calf, her forehead against its side, her eyes closed. She had never felt so tired.

Yaa, be merciful. Take this spirit, worthy of you, so my second mother might live.

Please.

The first flies were gathering on the carcass. Leya leaned against the calf's body to draw herself back up, mud squelching under her pads.

There was truth in the stories; she knew it. Why would she have seen a calf in the feverlands, if not for this moment, if not to guide her?

Thembe would live. This was what Leya was meant to do. It had all fallen into place.

Leya took the calabash to the last of the water. It would only fill partway in the shallow puddle, so she scooped up water in her palms and dribbled it in. She worked with a sudden certainty, a sudden peace. Thembe would live. The rains would come. She would see Bahati again someday. All would be well. She lifted the calabash and made the long walk back to camp.

Thembe died just after sunset.

She dreamed every night of the feverlands calf, and it spoke now with Thembe's voice, reciting the old stories, calling her sister, calling her daughter, calling her name.

It rained, now, every afternoon. The water hole filled and overflowed. Almost overnight the veld greened again, new grass pushing up, herds coming back to graze. Nanji and Masika went hunting. Leya stayed back. She still hadn't found her spear and had no heart to make another.

A dozen days after Thembe's death, Masika found Leya sitting outside the tents, wet to the skin from the steady rain.

"Leya, come inside."

Leya started shivering and couldn't stop. She stared at the pads of her hands, palm and fingertips, all stained red from rubbing the ochre into Thembe's body, marking the white lioness as one who now walked the spirit world. Leya had scrubbed her hands several times with grit and mud and stones, but the color remained. She wondered if it always would.

"Leya." Masika's voice broke through, sterner now. "I lost one of my sisters in the feverlands. I won't lose another there because of her own foolishness. Inside."

The last word sounded very like her mother's voice, and more from habit than obedience she rose and followed Masika into the *karanjala*'s tent. Masika rubbed Leya's fur dry with soft hides, as if she were ill or a child to be taken care of. Leya said nothing, made no move to hinder or help. But it had been nice, she thought, to feel cold that deep, first on the skin and then deeper. It was at least feeling something from outside herself, instead of feeling trapped inside her own mind.

Masika had two oil lamps burning in her tent, one for light and the other with a small pot suspended over it. She poured something from the pot into a small clay cup and handed the cup to Leya. "Drink this."

"What is it?"

"Just tea. It'll keep your strength up."

There was no honey in it, and the deep ruddy color reminded her of the ochre on her palms. But it was warm, and the earthy sweetness of it was pleasant, and without really meaning to she drank it all.

"There now, that's a good girl," Masika said, as if Leya were a toddling cub. She took the empty cup and wrapped a blanket of cape buffalo hide around Leya's shoulders.

Leya looked up. "Why didn't you tell me you and my mother were sisters?"

Masika's gaze grew distant a moment. "Because I promised her I wouldn't."

"Why?"

Masika took a cup of tea for herself. "She didn't want to encourage you. Not down this path, anyway. I told her you would find out eventually."

"She should be proud of you." *Of me.*

"I think she is, in her own way. But you should understand…" Masika stared into her cup a moment. "Our father always admired the *karanja*, and when it became clear early on that my path would lead me to them, he made no secret of his pride. And that hurt Naimah bitterly. She never truly believed it could be possible to love two children equally, for different reasons. She never believed that our parents could love a wife and mother as much as a huntress. And for many years it poisoned things between us."

Leya tried to imagine her mother feeling left out, frustrated, unloved. It was like stretching a muscle she hadn't known was there.

"But she's done the same thing to me. If she was upset because her path wasn't respected, why doesn't she respect mine now?"

Masika smiled sadly. "Some questions don't have answers. Count that one among them." She set her empty cup aside. "But she does care. Don't doubt that. She wouldn't have come out here to see you if she didn't."

"What?" Leya raced back through her memory, searching, finding nothing. "When?"

"That first time you came with us on the hunt," Masika reminded her. "She was out in the veld that night. She was the one who spooked the wildebeest. The others didn't see her, but I did. Or heard her, I should say." She shook her head. "For all I tried to teach her, she still walks like a damned elephant."

Leya let that settle in her mind, then stretched the new muscle again. Her mother as a sister. Her mother as a daughter. As a child. Like her, and not like her. Her own mind, her own heart.

Maybe it wasn't about her mother seeing her as a woman. Maybe it was about accepting her mother as one. Allowed to have faults. Allowed to be wrong. And worthy of love in spite of it all. Just as she was.

She remembered what Thembe had said, the boxes they were put into. Maybe the box of being Leya's mother, and no more, was as small as the one of being Naimah's child.

The rain drummed softly on the tent. Leya pulled the blanket tighter around her. It held Thembe's scent, sweet musk and strong, and she breathed it in deep, wanting to hold on to it just a while longer before it faded from everything, as if the white lioness had never been.

She looked up to see Masika's eyes shining with tears. The fur on her cheeks still held a faint red stain.

"I miss her too," Masika said softly. The corner of her mouth twitched, but Leya couldn't tell if she was trying to smile or trying not to weep. At last she sighed. "Zhenga would tell us that we have a sister in the spirit lands now, where none die and none suffer and the great powers that shaped the earth still move, and that we should be honored by that, and pleased. But I would rather have her here."

They sat together in silence for a long time, and in that space between speech there was something quiet and sacred and true. When Masika spoke again, her voice seemed not to break that silence but rise gently out of it.

"Do you know, Leya, why the *karanja* live apart, why we take no mates, bear no cubs?"

"It's always been that way. Hasn't it?"

Masika nodded. "We don't merely live a different life. The life makes us different. The mothers in the villages give life, build it up, tend it like a fire. That force goes out through them, out to the world.

"We take life. At best, our prey yield it to us. At worst, we wrest it from them. That marks us, as much as the scars we bear."

"But the villages couldn't live without the meat we take them. Isn't that life?"

"For them, yes. But not for us." Again the same sad smile. "Look at me, Leya. Look at the years I wear. Every scar I bear from horn or hoof or fang is life fighting me. Struggling as hard as it can against me, against what I would do, against what I have to do. Again and again and again."

Masika's eyes were quiet embers. "Only death comes through me. Only death comes through every *karanja*. We accept that. We take joy in spite of it. And Thembe knew it as well as any *karanja* who ever lived."

Leya held the blanket tight around her, huddled on Masika's grass mat. She wanted to try to say what she was feeling, but it was too confused, too hard to catch, a swarm of bees and each with a different voice.

All at once she saw the elephant, pale and whole. *Speak*, it said; *the words will come.*

Leya swallowed. "I don't think I can hunt anymore."

Masika watched her silently.

"It isn't that I can't kill. It's not that I don't have the stomach for it. But I can't be death and nothing else."

Because being *karanja* was a box, too, she realized. She had just never tested its size before, because she thought she'd fit. For a while she had, but now…

Her feverlands calf, under a net of twine.

Her soul a bird, struggling to get free.

She couldn't go back to her village, to any village. Masika was right; she was marked, by her scars without and within. There was no life for her among those huts again.

But was there any life for her here?

Then Masika spoke quietly, almost more to herself than to Leya.

"It is said that in times of great suffering, some among us would go out into the world for a time, to seek what there was to be sought. To live truly apart, until there was understanding within them. It has been a long time since any *karanja* has taken that path."

Masika turned, took up a spear, and placed it in Leya's hands—Leya's own spear, she realized, that she hadn't seen, hadn't held, since that last hunt.

"Perhaps," said Masika, "it's time now."

CHAPTER 4

A vulture flew lazy circles in the late afternoon sky. Leya squinted up at it for a moment, then turned her attention back to the veld and the scrub hare she'd killed. "Don't get your hopes up," she muttered. She was hungry enough after the day's walk that there wasn't going to be a scrap of it left.

She skinned and gutted the hare with swift, sure cuts, then skewered the carcass on a spit she'd cobbled together from branches and twine. It would probably turn out like most of her cooking, charred on the outside and nearly raw inside, but she told herself she was learning to like it that way. She'd left with only a few things in her pack—a small undyed tent, a clay oil lamp, twine, dried meat, her knife and spear—and a cooking-pot was one thing she'd forgotten.

It was her fifth day on the veld, and it was still strange to be out this far alone, with nowhere to be, nowhere to go back to because someone would expect her. Nothing was expected of her now, although Masika did advise her to send word from time to time either to her or to Naimah if there were any opportunity.

The first day, she'd mostly slept, surprising herself at how exhausted she'd been. The second day, she found a river and followed it. Once she'd seen, in the distance, a group of red tents—far more than Masika's *karanja*—but didn't go near. She would have been welcome at their fire, as Masika had told her, but something in her didn't want the huntress' company. Besides, they would likely want the news of Masika's band, and she didn't want to have to give it, not with the red ochre still on her palms.

By the time the rabbit was ready, the sun was dropping off the edge of the earth, and the first stars came out as she ate. It was a little more done inside than usual. Maybe she was learning. The elephant calf in her mind held its head high.

She wondered idly if the calf would grow as the seasons passed. She wondered if it really was a spirit or just something inside her that her mind had given an elephant's shape. And if it was a spirit, was it the same one from the feverlands, or had the mud-stuck calf's spirit lingered, with no rainspeaker to make sure it was released?

She tried asking it those questions but got no answer. She tried asking if it was male or female and heard nothing back either. Perhaps spirits were neither, or both. She was no rainspeaker to know. Sometimes the calf spoke, most of the time it didn't, but Leya found herself mentally talking to it on her journey, and something in that was comforting. If it spoke with Thembe's voice, maybe she was talking to Thembe's spirit. That hurt her and soothed her all at the same time.

She gazed out across the veld. There was no moon tonight in the clear sky, no light but starlight and her own small fire. Then she saw something else—a flicker of light at the horizon.

Another fire? She squinted at it. If it was a fire, it was no larger than hers. Someone else traveling alone, perhaps. She watched the light for a long time, feeling an odd kinship with whoever it was, wondering where they were going and why. She hoped they were going home, wherever home was, and there would be a welcome there, and rich food, and honey-beer to drink, and dancing.

She wasn't sure where her own home was anymore.

And when you start thinking those kinds of things, she told herself, *it's time to sleep.*

She smothered the fire, spread out her sleeping-mat in a patch of bare ground, and dozed off. When she woke briefly in the middle of the night, the other light in the distance was gone as well.

The sun was already up when she woke, and she felt disoriented at first, not sure where she was or when or why. She'd expected that feeling would go away after a few days, but so far it hadn't. This time, she felt as if she'd been dreaming, something vivid and not entirely pleasant, but none of the images remained, only a vague uneasiness that stayed with her as she got up to pack.

She almost stumbled over something sitting at the corner of her sleeping-mat.

A clay cooking-pot. Small. Just the right size for someone traveling alone.

Leya frowned. She stood and scanned the scrub around her, watching for movement. She smelled nothing. She sniffed the clay, but it smelled only of sweet grasses—perhaps it had been packed in them to keep from breaking on a journey.

It was a beautiful pot, and she turned it over and over in her hands, admiring the shape and heft of it. It was deep red, mostly, but there were other shades mingled with it, and the overall effect made her think of sunset, reds and oranges and even pink melting together. Who would give such a precious thing to a stranger, with nothing in return?

Leya looked around again, but there was still no sign of anyone, not even any tracks. That impressed her and frightened her at the same time. The *karanja* were known for moving silently on the veld, and she'd learned from the best at marking where prey had walked. Who could sneak up on a huntress, walk away, and leave no sign, no track, no scent?

A spirit? She shuddered, but the elephant calf spoke up and told her not to be a cub. Spirits couldn't work in the world of things you could touch.

She thought of the firelight she'd seen in the distance. But that was too far away—wasn't it?

There were no answers, so she tucked the question away in her mind. "Thank you," she said finally, out loud, in case they were still nearby. It felt silly, but it also felt right. Then she rolled the clay pot carefully in her sleeping-mat. Masika had given her a packet of the red tea to take with her, and tonight she could finally have some. She chewed a few bites of dried meat, drank from the river, and went on.

Each day that followed brought another gift. Some nights she saw the firelight in the distance, and some nights she didn't.

One morning she went to the river and found a sharp V freshly drawn in the mud, facing sideways. She puzzled over that until she went closer to drink and saw the crocodile, resting low in the water with only its eyes visible. There were no slide marks in the nearby mud; it must have come into the water elsewhere and swam farther down to wait for prey. If she hadn't known... Again, she spoke her thanks out loud but saw no sign of whoever had helped her.

The next day she came across a spot of bright orange amid the green grasses, wedged tight between two rocks in her path. A kiwano, just as she'd eaten with Nuru. She smiled and worked it free, wishing the person had stayed to share half of it with her. She'd eaten little but meat for days, and the crisp freshness of the melon cooled her mouth.

She wondered what Nuru was doing, whether he thought of her, whether he missed her. She was surprised she didn't think of him more often, despite a teasing dream here or there. She wished he were here now if only to make her laugh, to help her forget for a while, but she didn't long for his company otherwise. When they were together, it was pleasant. When they were apart, well... they were apart. There was no twine binding the two of them, real or unseen.

She thought of Nuru as a cub, left to be raised by someone else while his mother followed the herds. Of course he asked nothing of her, she realized; he was used to being left behind.

She thought of his easy laugh, his deep eyes, his deft touch. Nuru deserved more than a bond that lasted a night at a time. He deserved love, not just desire; devotion, not just passion that faded with sunrise. Whether he knew it or not, he deserved someone who would stay.

As do you, the elephant calf said.

Leya imagined herself spitting a seed at it.

回⚙回

The song woke her the next morning. At first she thought it was the wind whistling through the thorn-trees, but the sound was lower, warbling and sweet. She packed up quickly and followed it through the veld, heart racing.

At last she saw the source of it, perched cross-legged on a grouping of rocks: a painted dog, female, playing a wooden flute.

She was dressed in a hide skirt elaborately embroidered with beads, with other bits of bone and wood threaded through her right ear. Leya guessed the dog to be older than herself, though perhaps not as old as her mother or Masika. She had only ever seen the painted dogs once, when she was little, as a small pack of them crossed the veld when she was out foraging with her mother. There had been only six or seven of them, silhouetted against the blue sky. She'd heard they tended to stay together in packs of several families, moving from camp to camp with the herds instead of living in one village as her people did. What was this one doing all alone?

As Leya came closer, the dog winked at her and kept playing. The notes flowed out, turned back, then leapt like crickets as she blew short breaths into the flute. She finished with a single note, clear and sweet, fading it into the sound of the wind in the grass, as if the song had come from there to begin with. The very air seemed somehow richer, as if a song could linger like early fog.

The dog took the flute from her mouth and smiled down at Leya. "That's my dawn song," she said, her voice deep and slow. "Sometimes I put a wisp more cloud in it, but I thought this was a bright blue sort of day, don't you think?"

"It was beautiful."

"So was the dawn." The dog slipped down off the rock.

"It's been you, hasn't it? Leaving things?"

The dog grinned. "And it's been you finding them."

"That crocodile—"

"Oh, yes. That one's sneaky. Have to be careful with him. I have a song for him, too, but it's better played at night." The dog studied her a moment, head cocked slightly like she was listening to echoes of her song in the distance. "You're far from home, *karanja*. What brings you into these lands?"

"It's a long story."

"Good! You can tell me on the way. But we cannot travel as strangers. I am Ndiri. What do they call you, huntress?"

"Leya."

"Leya," Ndiri said, repeating the name like it was an expression of triumph. She clapped Leya on the shoulder, hard enough to startle her but not to hurt. "Now we are not strangers anymore, hey? And you can come to our home and eat with us, and I will make a song for you."

"Oh... I..."

Leya felt a sudden disdain from the elephant calf. Of course she had no other destination.

"I'd love that," Leya finished.

Ndiri was looking at her curiously. Leya's ears burned, but she told herself it wasn't as if the dog could hear her thoughts. Then Ndiri nodded. "Off we go, then." The dog glanced over her shoulder and whistled a high, sharp note through her teeth. "Mtoto! Time to go."

From among the shadows under the rocks, a little shape uncurled itself, stretched, and stood—a paint-dog pup, seven or eight rains old, wearing only a clay pendant with a symbol pressed into it.

"He doesn't speak many words," Ndiri said. "And it would take the great sun-mother herself to keep a loincloth on the boy. But he's smart, this one—and mostly good." She glared at the pup playfully, then grinned, showing white teeth, and the pup grinned back.

Leya followed the two across the veld, using trails she hadn't seen but that the dogs obviously knew by heart. There was no doubt now that the fire she'd seen had been theirs, even as far away as it was; both dog and pup moved at a surprisingly swift, loping pace, and both as silently as the *karanja*. When they stopped to rest through the heat of the day, Leya told them as much as she dared, about the *karanja*, about leaving for a journey to see new places, to be on her own for a while. She didn't mention Thembe, or Bahati, or the elephant calf, but somehow the shapes of them must have gotten into the spaces between her words, because often Ndiri looked as though she guessed a good deal of what Leya was careful not to say.

When there was nothing else for Leya to tell, Ndiri spoke of herself. She was a healer, it turned out, and skilled with birthing young, and those needs had her often running these trails, going from village to camp to family, doing her best to help whoever needed help. Her mother had been a healer before her, and her mother before that, and several generations before. Leya got vaguely dizzy just thinking of it.

"Did you make the cooking-pot? It's beautiful," she added, feeling how inadequate the word was. "It looks just like the sunset."

"It does. But no, that was not my work. I work in root and

leaf and song; my friend Shani works the earth. I take her pots to the big village sometimes, to trade for what we need. That one was left, and I was sad to have to take it back to her. But when I found you, I knew it was yours."

"I thought—at first—it was Kamara, leaving me gifts," Leya said shyly.

Ndiri leaned back and laughed, but there was no mockery in it, only a child's delight. "Oh, no, no, no. I am flesh and bone and blood and many mistakes and a little wisdom, enough perhaps to fill the very tip of my tail. And I hope not to be a spirit for a long, long time."

Leya found herself smiling. She had no idea what it was like to be with child, and no particular interest in finding out, but she thought if she were, she would want someone like Ndiri to help her at the birth. Ndiri's eyes were warm as embers, and she gave off life and joy and comfort like a fire gave off heat and light. Mtoto sat by quietly, watching, chewing on a bit of Leya's dried meat. She wished she had one of Bahati's toys to give him.

At last they reached a stand of baobab trees, and Ndiri paused before the largest one in the center. It was easily three times as big as the *aumah*'s hut in Leya's village, and ten villagers with arms outstretched could not have circled the bulbous trunk.

"You... live here?"

Ndiri grinned. "The land provides."

Mtoto ran ahead of them, disappearing into an entrance in one side. A moment later, someone else came out, a small, slender golden jackal female—or at least, that was what Leya thought she was, though it was hard to see the golden fur under streaks of red clay that covered her arms and belly and beaded skirt. It looked like the jackal had fought a mudhole and lost.

Ndiri groaned. "Shani! I bring home a new friend for

us, and this is how you look?" She turned back to Leya and winked. "You see I have to play mother to this one too."

Inside the tree it was shady and cool. The trunk had almost formed chambers as it hollowed out, creating little nooks here and there, so different from the simple round huts and open tents Leya was used to. She felt not merely sheltered by the tree but protected by it, surrounded by its strong, ancient wood, by something that still lived. She put a hand to the rough interior of the trunk and imagined she could feel it growing, and the elephant calf in her mind stood still and silent, as if it felt the same wonder. This tree might have been a seedling in the long time before, when Kamara herself had walked the land.

As her eyes adjusted to the light, she saw other details: baskets and tools hanging from pegs in the bark, places where the interior had been carved or painted with shapes of prey or just curving lines and colors. Clay pots sat tucked into crevices, and sacks of coarse fibrous cloth were piled here and there. It wasn't neat, but it wasn't cluttered, and everything seemed to belong.

Ndiri brought her clear water that tasted faintly of wood and something sharp and sweet, and then she brought out little cakes of mashed baobab fruit Shani had made to welcome them home.

"I'm so glad I made plenty!" Shani said. "If there weren't enough," she added to Leya, "I would have given you mine, of course. But then I wouldn't have had any."

The jackal was an amusing contrast to Ndiri, Leya found. Where Ndiri was deliberate and calm, Shani bubbled and yipped. If Ndiri was a song, Shani was a dance, stepping lightly on dainty feet in a circle around Leya, sniffing at her pack, her necklace, the nape of her neck.

Ndiri sighed. "You mustn't mind Shani. She's..." The dog searched for the right word, then shrugged. "She's Shani."

"Oh!" Shani stopped suddenly. "I need a song." She dashed outside a moment, then came back carrying a pot almost as big as she was, its surface polished to a shiny brown so dark it was almost black.

"My," Ndiri said. "That's a fine one there."

Shani beamed, jumping up and down in place. "I know, isn't it? Isn't it lovely? It's my very best. But it needs a song. It won't be done without it."

Ndiri nodded. "I will play it my night song."

"Oh, good. I hope it's a good big song, though. It can hold a lot of the night, I think."

Ndiri smiled tenderly. "I will play it all the stars. That will fill it up."

After they had finished eating, Ndiri took her flute out again. This time, the song was low and steady, sweeping and vast, each note played until there was nothing more left of it, and then the next, like breathing deep and slow in sleep.

Leya thought of that night with Bahati, before her initiation, the night he'd first given her the bracelet, the stars stretched out over them. She thought of the night they had spent together later, the feeling of his body on hers. It was all there in the song, not what had happened, but the way it had all felt in her, the vastness of it, the depth, the wonder.

The last note faded slowly, softly, like a mother putting a cub to bed. Even Shani was still and quiet for a moment after. Then she peeked into the small hole at the top of the pot.

"Perfect," she said happily, and Leya agreed.

It was a strange sort of family, Leya thought, but somehow she found herself fitting perfectly into it. There was never talk of her leaving, never any suggestion that she might not stay, and so she did.

She had never been among anyone, not even rainspeak-ers, who spoke the way Ndiri and Shani did about things. Leya had always thought only creatures had spirits, as she was taught, but Ndiri and Shani spoke of the earth and the water and firewood as if everything were alive and listening. Sometimes it made her laugh, sometimes it made her think, and sometimes it simply blew over her like the wind, some-thing just there, that didn't need to be understood.

They lived, it seemed, almost entirely on the fruit of the baobab that hung down straight from the branches. They ate meat when they could, but they traded for it. She never quite understood their explanation why neither of them hunted—that it spoiled the songs, spoiled the clay—but they didn't hold her skills against her, and all three eagerly ate the light meat she snared in the lands around their home. There were herds that moved in those lands, but though she watched them, she went no closer, and she left her spear at the tree. The elephant calf in her mind grew quiet, but it didn't seem displeased, only resting as a silent, familiar presence, like a friend sitting with her at the fire.

She helped Shani gather clay at the riverbank, watching for crocodiles and carrying back more than the slim jackal could manage alone. In return, Shani let her try shaping the clay. It was cool and slick under her pads, and though the little cup she made was uneven and tilted, Shani acted as if she'd made something as grand as the big star-filled pot. With anyone else, Leya would have suspected she was being teased, but as light-hearted as Shani was, she wore no masks. They put Leya's cup with the other pieces, to be fired, as Shani called it, in a stone oven just beyond the trees. Once the clay was hard, Leya clumsily painted it red, to try to match her cooking-pot, and Shani fired it again and polished it smooth. Leya drank from it every day from then on. It wasn't perfect, but it was hers.

Another day she found Shani sitting with a lump of clay before her, just staring at it, as if it were telling a story and she was listening.

"What are you doing?" Leya asked.

"Waiting."

"For what?"

"For it to tell me what it is. Doesn't want to talk today. Might just have to try." She shaped a cup, cocked her head at it. "No, no, no." She pressed it down, started again, waited, whined softly, and shook her head again.

"But you can make it anything you want, can't you?" Leya asked.

"Oh, no, no. Some clay is cups. Some clay is pots. Some clay is beads or little hippos for Mtoto. All different."

Leya shrugged. "Maybe that just wants to be clay."

Shani cocked her head at the lump of clay again. "Yes," she said finally. "I think so." And she carried it back to the river and set it down and tenderly patted it in. Leya told Ndiri about it later, and the dog sighed but smiled.

Some days, though, the clay said nothing. One morning Leya woke to find Shani sitting outside under one of the other trees, crying silently. Mtoto sat beside her, leaning against the jackal as if she were a tree herself. Worried, Leya found Ndiri, but the dog only nodded slightly.

"She gets sad sometimes," Ndiri said. "Leave her be, and it'll pass."

And the next morning, it was as if nothing had happened. Shani went back to work on a new pot, chattering happily to it and Mtoto and Leya.

That afternoon, Leya was sitting outside roasting another scrub hare for their evening meal when she saw someone approaching at a run. A lion—either a female or a young male; it was hard to tell at first. When the figure reached the baobabs, she saw it was a female, barely half-grown, her chest still flat. As the lioness caught her breath, her eyes widened at the sight of Leya, lingering on the scars.

"Ndiri?" the lioness whispered.

Ndiri came out then, embracing the lion briefly. "Your mother?"

The lioness nodded, still getting her breath back. "Waters broke yesterday. All night—and it doesn't come."

"Can you see the head?"

"Yes, but no more. Alive or dead, we don't know."

Ndiri nodded. "Rest while I get my things, and we will go."

The young lioness leaned against a tree, eyeing Leya. It was the first time, Leya realized, that anyone here had looked at her as a stranger. She brought a small cup of water, and the lioness sipped at it slowly while they waited.

By the time the cup was empty, Ndiri had returned, carrying her pack, and Leya was surprised to see Mtoto with her.

"Should I come with you?" Leya asked, worried that Mtoto might not be able to keep up in such a hurry.

"If you like," Ndiri said, and they set off.

Despite his short legs, Mtoto had less trouble staying close to Ndiri than Leya and the young lioness did. Even so, the healer arrived in the village several minutes before Leya and Mtoto, and the young lioness led them to the hut where Ndiri already knelt at the mother's thighs.

Leya was struck by how much it looked like her own village, the same size, the same mud and grass style used to build the huts. Even inside the mother's hut, it looked very like her own, and somewhere she even smelled safou cakes cooking.

Ndiri rubbed her hands with oil and slid them inside the mother's body, feeling carefully, her head cocked a bit like Shani listening to the clay. Then she grunted softly, a sound of satisfaction, and withdrew. "Good position," she said, relief obvious in her voice. "Just needs a bit of help, this one. We all need help sometimes—this one just starts early, hey?" She smiled reassuringly at the mother, and the exhausted lioness managed a slight smile back.

A certain calm settled over the hut, even when the pains began again and the mother cried out, even with the smell of blood and birth strong in the air. Leya marveled at Ndiri's stillness and the steadiness of her hands. Every moment was precise, sure, and gentle as she spoke quiet instructions to the mother and guided the cub out. Leya hadn't realized she'd been holding her breath until the cub cried.

Ndiri tied the cord, cut it with a bone-handled knife, and led them through passage of the afterbirth, telling the young lioness how to bury it, where, and what to say over it. At last she washed mother and child with water Mtoto had fetched without being told, then set about steeping a tonic to help the mother's milk.

Leya watched it all in silent wonder. It was like watching a dance—or a hunt, in its own way. She tried to put it into words as they left the mother's hut, but she couldn't find the ones to say what she was feeling, and Ndiri only nodded.

"It was a good birth," the healer said. "Sometimes they are not so easy. Come; we have others to see."

Leya and Mtoto followed as Ndiri went to tend to several other villagers. Leya caught whispers here and there, surely wondering why a *karanja* walked with the healer, but she paid no attention, too caught up in Ndiri's work.

A young male who'd been ill at the last rains was found strong and well again. He joked with Ndiri about how bad her medicine had tasted, and his mother pressed a basket of grouse eggs into Ndiri's hands, despite the healer's protests.

Next Ndiri looked in on an older male, lying thin and weak on his mat, a young cub using a zebra-tail whisk to keep the flies from his eyes and mouth as he slept. Outside the hut, Ndiri took the male's older daughter aside and spoke to her softly, and left them with a packet of herbs for his pain.

"He won't see the next full moon," Ndiri told Leya quietly as they left, "but what I gave will ease his passing."

She left baobab fruit at another hut with fussy twin cubs, with instructions to mix the pulp with water to soothe their stomachs. "Never hurts and usually helps," she told Leya. "Sometimes that's the best you get." There, she was paid with a small woven sack of grain. Ndiri never asked for anything, but most gave food or some small item in return.

Later, as they rested in the veld on their way home, Leya asked the question that had shadowed her all day. "What do you use for fever?"

"What kind of fever?"

"After a wound, when it gets red and smells bad. When…" She swallowed hard. "When they can't get their breath anymore, and nothing can keep them cool."

"That is bad. But I think I would use these." She took out roots and gray powder. "They are strong, but they don't always work."

Leya sniffed the medicines carefully. It didn't smell like anything Zhenga had used. Maybe they didn't grow in the *karanja*'s lands. But if they had… She stared at them in her palm. Would these have kept Thembe alive, when the elephant calf's spirit could not? She looked up and saw Ndiri watching her.

"Once the song is played," Ndiri said, "you cannot call the notes back."

They ate then, roasting some of the grouse eggs and finishing with a few strips of dried meat. Ndiri took out two little clay hippos and gave them to Mtoto, and he set about digging a hole and pouring water into it to make mud for them to wallow in.

Leya watched him, wondering what worlds went through

his mind that he couldn't tell them about. She remembered, suddenly, what Ndiri had said when Shani had come out to meet them—that she played mother to Shani, too.

Too. She'd assumed all along that Mtoto was Ndiri's son, but now she wasn't sure. She wanted to ask, but there didn't seem to be a polite way. She tried out several questions in her mind, then spoke. "Have you always traveled alone?"

Ndiri stretched. "Not always. I ran with my pack even as a healer, for a long time, until I was older than you."

"Why did you leave?"

Ndiri nodded toward Mtoto, who was making happy bubbling noises as he pressed the toy hippos into the mud. "I helped with his birth, in another pack. He was early, and small, and they knew his scent was wrong." Ndiri was quiet a moment. "So they left him."

"Left him?"

"On the veld." She met Leya's gaze calmly. "Yes. To die. As is the custom. So I took him, and I became his mother. I had no milk to give him, but I fed him on the seeds of egusi ground into water and honey, and he grew strong.

"And for that," Ndiri finished, "I was driven out, and no other pack would take me, because I had broken their law and so tempted evil spirits to bring bad luck to my people."

Ndiri looked back at Mtoto and smiled, watching him play. "And I would do it a hundred times over again. For his sake, and for mine."

They sat in silence for a time after that. Leya felt like she should say something too, something in return, about Thembe, about Bahati, about the elephant calf she still saw every day. Ndiri had been so open, she deserved some of the secrets Leya was keeping, the way she deserved the food and the baskets the villagers gave her, even though she didn't ask for them.

"I didn't leave the *karanja* because I wanted to see the

land," Leya began.

Ndiri nodded.

"I don't know where I belong. I haven't for—a long time. I left to try to find out. Everything I wanted—if I chose one thing, I couldn't have the other. And then I didn't even feel like it was my choice anymore. Like anything was my choice anymore."

Ndiri nodded. "Every time you take a step toward something, you take a step away from something else. Sometimes you know it. Sometimes you don't. But," and she smiled, "the trick is not to step away from *everything* else."

Leya tried to grasp that. "There's so much more I haven't told you."

"I know."

"I should, though."

"If the right time comes, you will. If that time does not come, that is all right. We all carry things in us others never see. Secrets are not always bad."

Leya sought out the feverlands calf in her mind. It skin shone bright and strong. It seemed content. She nodded.

Ndiri took out her flute then and played. She played the birth they had seen, the first days of the cub's life, the last days of the male's. She played strength coming back from weakness, and the joy at being able simply to stand, to run, to take pleasure in eating. She played gratitude, golden and sweet.

It was like bathing her mind in clear water, like wind blowing dust from her spirit. Leya felt tired but satisfied, hollowed but washed clean.

"Good to have a song after the work," Ndiri explained, packing the flute away. "Puts everything back in its place again."

Leya thought of the births that weren't so easy, the times where there was nothing to do but ease death. She knew she'd seen very little of what Ndiri's work truly meant. She wanted to ask how Ndiri did it, how she went on, how the darkness didn't swallow her up when only death came through her. If Leya could learn that, if she could find that calm, still place within her that Ndiri seemed to call forth at will, then maybe she could be a *karanja* again.

She remembered something else as they doused their fire, gathered up Mtoto's hippos, and found the trail again. "That first day when we met—you said you would play my song."

"And I will. But I can't yet." Ndiri clapped her on the shoulder and grinned, tongue lolling. "I'm still learning it."

回 ۞ 回

The next day, Leya and Ndiri were sitting outside while Shani polished a small cooking-pot, rubbing the surface until it shone as if it were wet. Ndiri was grinding dried herbs into powder between two stones, and Leya held the little cloth bags they went into. Ndiri had told her what they were for, when to use them, when not to use them, how to mix them with water or porridge. She showed Leya how to knot the bags shut in a particular way to mark what was in them. Leya thought of the hand signals the *karanja* used, and marveled at the ways knowledge could be held and passed.

After a time, the steady scraping rub of Shani's polishing stopped, and they saw the jackal staring at the side of the tree, where Leya had left her spear propped against the trunk.

"Your spear is sad," Shani said.

Just when Leya thought she was used to the things Shani said, the jackal came up with something new. "Sad?" Leya echoed.

Shani nodded. "Sad."

Leya looked at Ndiri. Ndiri shrugged and went back to grinding the leaves.

"How is my spear sad?"

"Because you're not using it. Things like to be used. They're sad when they're not."

"I *am* using it. I used it for that hare you ate this morning."

"But that's not why you made it. You made it for big things," Shani explained. "It wants big things."

Leya tried to think of something of say.

"It's also very plain," Shani said, studying it. "It needs something. Can I give it something?"

Yaa's whiskers. Leya imagined the spear splashed with bright paint or with the shaft whittled to a toothpick. With Shani, anything was possible. She only hoped she'd still be able to hunt with it when it was done. "Well… All right."

Shani yipped like a pup, grabbed the spear, and dashed inside, leaving the pot forgotten.

"She's right, you know," Ndiri said after a moment.

"That my spear is sad?" Leya bit back laughter.

Ndiri did laugh. "Maybe not quite that part. But it was made to hunt among the herds. And that is part of you, too."

Leya remembered the dark, clear nights, the scent of zebra and impala sharp on the wind. The pounding of her heart, waiting for the signal, for the right moment to test her aim and her strength. She knew her throwing-arm was getting weak, and she'd tried to tell herself it didn't matter, but it did.

Because it *was* part of her. Even now, on the moonless nights, she looked out across the veld sometimes and felt that wind and sky and earth pulling her to it.

But she couldn't tell Ndiri about the useless fear that rose up in her now, how she could only see horns and hooves where once she saw meat and blood. With the thump of hooves and the grinding of grass on flat teeth came also the sight of Thembe on the ground, belly torn open. Her gasping breaths. The heat of her pads. And the great cold stillness that followed.

It was not the great game she'd thought it to be so long ago.

"I don't know," Leya said.

"Well. First we will see if you still have a spear, when she is finished." Ndiri winked at her and went back to work.

Shani worked on the spear for two days. She was determined to keep it a surprise, so Leya stayed away while Shani worked on it, and Shani covered it carefully with a cloth when they were all inside.

At last, after a breakfast of porridge and melon, Shani brought the spear outside, holding it behind her back. Leya surreptitiously tried to tilt her head to see it; at least the point and the far end of the shaft looked the same. At last, eyes brimming with excitement, Shani held it out to her.

Leya took it. Held it. Stared at it.

In the center of the shaft, perfectly balanced, was a tiny clay figure of an elephant, detailed down to a bright black eye and the grooves of its skin. It was tied securely to the wood with twine, and the twine had been dyed with red ochre. The twine continued just far enough down the shaft to give her a good grip, but not so far that it wouldn't fly easily off her fingers when she threw it.

Leya's throat closed. The elephant calf in her head trumpeted, a sound she had never heard it make. It sounded twice as big as it looked.

"Is it good?" Shani bounced on her tiptoes. "If it isn't good, I can try again. I *felt* like it was good. I really did."

Leya thought of what she'd expected the spear to look like, and the laugh bubbled up all on its own. Somewhere in the veld of her mind, cool rain fell, and the thirsty earth soaked it up and greened again.

"Yes, it's good," she said, when she could speak. "It's perfect."

"It's so happy now. Can you feel it?"

Leya nodded. "Yes. I can." She looked at the sky. The night would be clear. The moon was almost full. And now, holding this spear, she knew she could do it again. Not the same as before, not so easy and thoughtless as before, but that was all right. In its way, it would be better than before.

It was a good night, Leya thought, for a hunt.

She had already forgotten most of the old chant the *karan-ja* used as they brought a fresh kill to the village, but as Leya carried the pink-red meat over her head, the tattered striped hide fluttering behind, she repeated the parts she knew over and over, and the feeling was the same. She had dreamed as a cub of bringing a kill this way, and though the village was a stand of baobab trees and the villagers only Ndiri and Mtoto and Shani, that feeling was the same, too.

Ndiri had been right; secrets weren't all bad. She wouldn't tell them how this evening she looked at the herds in a way she never had before, how she realized she took the weak and sick to make the herd stronger. She wouldn't tell them that through the elephant calf, she felt a strange kinship with the zebra she brought down, felt its spirit touch hers, lightly, yielding as its body yielded to her blade, and that she wept for it, and for Thembe, and for herself, as she never had before, until she was hollow and clean and whole again. She knew, now, that one day her memories would be sweetness instead of pain. And she knew, now, that she had the strength to live until that day.

It was a lot to learn in the space between a spear's throw and its landing. It was a lot to know in the space between the cut of a blade and the last rattling breath. She felt as if a hundred rains had come and passed in a single night.

She would not have said she was happy again, not exactly. But she carried, now, a certainty that she *could* be, and for now it was enough.

Shani squealed at the sight of her, though Leya wasn't sure whether it was because of her or because of the meat. The jackal ran to Ndiri. "Full moon tonight, Ndiri."

"Is it?" Ndiri glanced at the night sky with feigned indifference. "I hadn't noticed."

"It is, it is, it is! Can we build the fire? Please? We haven't since Leya came. And we have meat. Lots of meat. Full moon dance, *please*?"

"All right, all right. But you will help gather the wood."

A lot of wood, Leya found out, to build a fire as big as the ones in her village. Ndiri added oil in the right places, so that when the first spark touched the wood it blazed up bright all at once, and Shani clapped her hands and laughed to see it.

Ndiri brought out drums then, a large one stretched with hide for her and a smaller clay one for Mtoto, and they played, and Shani danced, spinning around the fire, so close to the flames sometimes that Leya worried she'd set her fur alight.

"Leya, come dance!"

"I... No—I don't."

"Yes, you do." Shani grabbed her wrist and tugged. "Can't you feel it?"

At first she just mimicked Shani's movements, but then bit by bit things fell away. She found a rhythm inside herself that matched the drums. She found a rhythm that matched the zebra, and the moon, and the night, that matched blood and stars. The tight fist of her body unclenched, and in her mind even the elephant calf picked up its feet and swayed in time. Shani spun her in circles until they were both dizzy and laughing, and they fell into the grass at the fire-circle's edge, and then the dance was over, and the only drumming left was their own racing hearts.

They cut the zebra meat in great chunks then and roasted it slow at the coals, and some of the meat they ate that way and some went into a stew with beans and seed pods and grain, to simmer for when they were hungry again later, though Leya couldn't imagine feeling hungry again for days. Mtoto fell asleep, curled up against Ndiri with a chunk of meat still in his fist, and she stroked his fur slowly.

"Now we need a story," Shani said.

They looked at Leya, and it took a moment for her to understand. "Me?"

"You are *karanja*, hey?" Ndiri gestured at what remained of the zebra. "Tell us a story of Kamara."

Leya's mouth had gone dry, and she took a gulp of water. She closed her eyes a moment.

You know the one, the calf whispered.

Leya opened her eyes. "Once, in the long time before, Kamara the Huntress had a sister. And from the time they were cubs they were always together, and they were like one spirit broken in two."

She tried to tell it as Thembe had, tried to match her voice to the rhythms of the words. Line by line, the story came back, and for a moment she was reciting it to Thembe again, with the rain drumming on the tent while Thembe threaded beads onto the necklace she still wore.

And then something changed. She knew the next line, where Kamara approached the calf, just before its mother appeared to stop her. Instead of those words, though, she heard herself say something different.

"Her blade struck deep into the calf, and its spirit filled her, like a calabash filled until the water flows over its sides and runs into the ground. She was filled with the spirit of the elephant, and the vastness of it touched her. And she was full of grief for what she'd done, for now that she knew its spirit, she loved the elephant even as she loved her sister."

She was weeping now, and she didn't understand why, but she went on. "And she knew, then, that it was not her choice who lived or died. She knew that in that matter she herself was no more than a spear to be thrown. And she prayed to Yaa to spare them both, and not punish them for her ignorance. And in his mercy he did. But ever after there was a bit of her sister's spirit in the elephant's, and a bit of the elephant's in her sister." Leya finished in a whisper. "As it has been, ever since."

No one spoke. The fire cracked and snapped. Slowly Leya came back to herself, feeling as if she'd been asleep and dreaming. "I don't..." She shook her head. "That's not how it goes."

"Stories change," Ndiri said, and somehow Leya felt she understood.

"And now a song!" Shani looked eagerly at Ndiri. "Something special."

"Oh, it is. Very special." Ndiri took up her flute. "I play Leya's song tonight."

Leya looked up, startled. Ndiri winked at her and put the flute to her mouth.

The song started soft, with stumbling notes like a cub learning to walk. Then they grew steadier, surer. The melody wandered, took a new direction, turned back, echoed itself faintly, and came back strong again.

Leya realized she was holding her breath, as she had been during the birth. The elephant calf waited along with her, open and listening.

There was a hesitation, a halted breath that was almost a mistake. And then the song soared, melody rising clear and strong and bright. She was the bird again in the feverlands, flying into endless blue. The last notes trailed off like a question. It felt unfinished, but that was right, too.

Shani murmured in the silence, a low sound of admiration. Leya said nothing, but when her gaze met Ndiri's, she winked at the dog and grinned.

Rains came and passed. Leya hunted often now, big things and small things, and the meat went to the villages along with Shani's pots and the skills of Ndiri's steady hands. In return, Ndiri agreed to teach Leya what she knew, and as the moon waned and waxed and waned again, she learned that the seeds of the cacana were poisonous but the fruit made an excellent poultice for burns, that the bark of the stinkwood was a good tonic for older males, and that a little purple flower she'd always admired turned out to be the best thing to soothe a cough. There was more than Leya felt she could learn in a lifetime, but she longed for however much she could hold. In time, Ndiri looked to Leya when they visited the villages and asked her what herb or tonic she would use. More and more often, their answers matched, and the day when Leya eased a cub's fever all on her own, she felt as proud and trembling and overwhelmed as the day she'd brought down the zebra to become a *karanja*.

As soon as she was able, Leya sent word to her mother, hoping her message would also reach Masika. She was well, she said, but would not be returning yet. She wasn't sure if she ever would, though she didn't tell them that. She missed the *karanja*, especially Masika, but there was a sisterhood here among the baobabs too, and no one had to cut away any part of herself to belong.

She was entirely unprepared when the moment came.

A new village, farther than they had ever traveled before. The same huts, the same fire-circle, the same sorts of faces around it.

Except for one.

He stood at the edge of the huts, two cubs with him. Golden mane, golden eyes, patient and warm, showing them how to spin the roarer on its twine to make the noise. At last the cub did it, and he laughed and picked the cub up and held it high before setting it safely back down.

Something in her shattered. Of course they were his. Look at him, in his prime now, no trace about him of the awkward half-maned male he had been. Of course he'd found the family he'd always wanted.

She wanted to say his name but couldn't speak. She wanted to run to him, embrace him, bury her nose in that mane again. She wanted to throw the sack of baobab fruit she carried as hard as she could at his head. She couldn't decide which one to do, so she just stood there and stared.

Ndiri was beside her. She tried to remember who Ndiri was. The dog took the sack from her, gently opening Leya's hands to free it. "Stories change," Ndiri whispered, and then she was gone.

He saw her then. She watched his eyes but couldn't tell what he felt. "Leya." Surprise. Amazement. Pleasure?

At last her tongue unlocked. "Bahati."

"Leya." A whisper.

The cubs had run off. They were alone now, an arm's length of space between them. She wanted desperately to cross it but didn't.

"I've missed you," she said.

Such love in his eyes. Such pain. "I'm sorry."

They went out into the veld then, as they always had, and though they were both far from home, it was somehow the same veld, the same rocks they sat on, the same great stretching sky above them.

She didn't have to ask the question; it was already in the air between them. Still, she gave it shape. "Why did you leave?"

A long moment passed. "I couldn't be what you needed me to be. I couldn't be... a toy, to be put aside and picked up again later. I wanted to be in your life, but I knew I wanted more than you could give. And I didn't want to be the reason you couldn't be happy, but I couldn't stop loving you. Couldn't stop wanting more."

He sighed, staring at the sky, not looking at her. "So I left. And I hurt you anyway. I just thought, if you didn't love me anymore, you could be... what you wanted to be." He shrugged, and now he looked like the young male had been, and she ached to see it.

Don't be too hard on him. Thembe's voice? The elephant's? Her own?

Perhaps all three.

And perhaps that went for herself as well.

"It's all right," she said.

"No, it isn't."

She grasped his hand with hers. "It is now." She paused. "The cubs... They were cute."

He relaxed, smiled. "Aren't they? Brothers four rains apart, but they look like twins."

"I'm happy for you," she said, and it was mostly true.

He frowned, confused.

"The cubs." Yaa's whiskers, did she have to say it straight out? "Your sons."

She had forgotten his laugh, the easy joy of it. For a moment she didn't even mind that he seemed to be laughing at her. "Leya, they're not mine."

"They're not?"

"Their father died a while back. They like me, so I try to... fill in where I can. That's all." He paused, grinning. "I'm not married either, to save you asking."

"But..." Leya tried to remember words, sounds, breath. "Why?"

Bahati's voice softened. "Because I love you."

She moved closer. How she'd missed this, the warmth of him against her, so familiar and always so new. She felt the elephant calf retreat to the farthest corner of her mind.

He spoke her name like a blessing and brushed his fingertips over her cheek, her throat, her smooth chest. No hesitation, no uncertainty. Blood rose in them both, and his scent warmed with hers, and there was nothing between them.

Later, she would tell him everything, life and death and life again, spirits and songs and secrets.

For now, she whispered his name in return, and touched her tongue to his, and drew his loincloth aside.

□ ☼ □

When she sought the elephant calf in her mind the next morning, she was surprised to see it larger, a juvenile now instead of a calf, even to the point of cutting tusks. It was proud of itself, and content, and Leya smiled at it, then rested her head on Bahati's chest and listened to the slow drum of his heart.

She was still *karanja*. She would always be that. But maybe she could be something else too. Something different. Something more.

The thought startled her, so simple, so new, so right. If she could find a way to take a step toward something without taking a step away from everything else—

She could be a huntress. A healer. A wife.

And if others could choose as well…

A *karanja* couldn't nurse a cub, but there was always the seed of the egusi.

But would they still be *karanja* then, tied to mates, to cubs? Or would they be something new? Could she hold on to what was good in that world, and bring it along to a new one?

Bahati stirred, and they held each other. "I was dreaming," he murmured.

"About what?"

"A bird. Under a net. I tried to get it free, but I couldn't undo the knots. And then it bit through the net and flew, and I thought it was gone, but it landed on my hand." He stretched out his hand, to show her.

She snuggled close. "Sounds like a good dream."

"It was."

Bahati went back to sleep then, but Leya lay awake, thoughts circling, mind alive with possibility. It might take a lifetime. It might take longer. She couldn't grasp it all yet; it was too much, too big, too wide to see the edges of, like the sky. She couldn't understand what it would mean, not yet.

You will sometime, the elephant whispered in Thembe's voice. *Just hold on to it.*

So she did.

CHAPTER 5

The sky over the village of Lwazi was crimson with sunset as the lionesses neared the mud huts. Already the great fire blazed in the circle, sending orange embers into the night, and around it the villagers were gathering, carrying baskets and cooking-pots and calabashes of beer.

Leya paused a moment, tasting the scene, the warm ruddy light amid the huts with the great vast darkness of the veld beyond. At the fire, there would be laughter and song and stories, old friends and new ones, all of it welcome as rain on dry earth to the travelers who followed the herds.

She felt the elephant in her mind sway back and forth, trunk swinging in anticipation. *Yes,* she said, *I will tell your story tonight.* The elephant was long of tusk now and carried the sky on its shoulders, but sometimes it still acted like a calf. Leya felt the same way—especially when she caught the scent of warm safou cakes at the fireside. Naimah had strength for little these days, but somehow a basket of the cakes was always waiting when Leya arrived.

Bahati caught up with her then, threading his fingers through hers as they walked toward the fire. The flickering light, all highlights and shadows, played tricks on her eyes, and for a moment she saw the cub he had been, the elder he would become, and at last the lion he was now, strong and wise and kind, the husband she loved, living at her side where he belonged, as she belonged at his.

"Are you drumming tonight?" she asked.

"Depends. Are you dancing?"

"Depends," she teased back. "Are you watching?"

"I might lose the rhythm."

"You might find one."

He brushed the back of her hand with his muzzle, smiled, and went to help the others prepare. Their last trail had been to the baobabs, and they'd left with a dozen pots to trade—a few of them Shani's, but most made by Mtoto now, who seemed to be as good or better at hearing what the clay wanted to be. The great tree was not the same without Ndiri, but something of the painted dog still lingered in the wood and the water and the wind, a song that was still playing, that would go on always.

Something of her lived elsewhere as well. Leya looked back at them, lionesses young and old, whole and cut, some with mates, some without, one with a new cub held close in a sling. They were the *ndiri*, huntresses and healers, workers of song and story. Sisters of the elephant. Bringers of life. Her sisters, her daughters, her aunts, every one. It had been a long birth and a hard one, but at last the *ndiri* were taking their first steps, speaking their first words, and Leya was as proud of all of them as any mother could be.

A slim, dark-eyed lioness approached, her hide skirt jangling with beads. "*Masika*, we're ready. Their *aumah's* waiting."

Leya had just opened her mouth to reply when something struck her heel. She frowned, knelt, and picked it up. A small stick, carefully polished, carved to a blunted point.

She looked at the other lioness. The expression she saw was a familiar one, that laughter in red-brown eyes. When Nuru's daughter had come to join the *ndiri*, there had been no question who her father was.

"I'll be right there," Leya said, and the lioness nodded and ran ahead.

Leya turned slowly, searching the shadows, hardening the line of her jaw. "You know I can see you," she called out. "Will you make me hunt you?"

She saw one cub, a little male, dart off into the night. A second came forward, female, eyes wide.

For a moment, their places were reversed, the girl-cub

and the leader, and Leya looked up at herself, the mane of fish-eagle feathers, the necklace of bone and hoof and ivory. The huntress, fierce and proud.

She wondered if Masika had ever been trying not to laugh.

Leya held up the stick. "Did you throw this?"

The cub jerked a nod.

Leya studied the stick, ran the pads of her fingers along it, and tested the blunt point with her thumb. "Hold out your hands."

The cub obeyed, and though her hands trembled, she met Leya's gaze.

Leya knelt down and laid the stick gently into the cub's hands. "You have a strong arm, little one. But practice first on things that don't hurt when you strike them. All right?"

The cub nodded, then drew a breath and found her voice. "I'm coming with you. When I'm bigger."

"You must be very strong, then, and very wise, and very kind. Can you be all those things?"

The cub's words ran out, so she shrugged, and Leya laughed. "There'll be plenty of time to find out." Leya stood. "Now, we'd better get to the fire. I smell safou cakes, and they'll all be gone if we don't hurry."

The first drums were already sounding in the night, humming in Leya's chest, her breath, her blood. Like the rumbling of elephants far in the distance. Like a story waiting to be told.

The cub scampered on ahead, into the firelight, where her family was waiting.

The huntress followed.

THE SHAPE OF THE SKY

Mtoto never tired of sunrise. Each day it was both familiar and different, comforting and dazzling. Some were quiet washes of color, the sky lightening so slowly you almost didn't realize the sunrise was happening until it was over. Others were loud, dramatic splashes of pink and orange that made the sky feel twice its size. Ndiri had always said that the sunrise was the first notes of a new day's song, and even when he was a child with her, they had watched them together. Now he watched them alone.

The young dog stretched, enjoying the soft breeze on his fur and how the warmth of the sun came back when the breeze stopped. As he preferred, he wore only the clay amulet he'd had since he was born. When he went among the villages to trade his pots and cups, he tied on a loincloth to respect their customs, but here among the baobabs, there was no custom but his own.

He uncovered the night's coals, built a small fire, and cooked his porridge. A little lilac-breasted roller landed nearby and hopped over to investigate, and he tossed the bird one of the dry grains.

Don't you get lonely out there, all by yourself?

That was what they always asked him in the village, whether he went among dogs or lions or anyone else. He always shook his head. He could see they didn't understand,

and he knew he couldn't explain it to them. He could tell they felt sorry for them, and sometimes that made him angry, even though he told himself they didn't—couldn't—know any better.

They already thought him strange because he spoke so little. It wasn't that he couldn't speak, as some had thought at first. He simply preferred to say what was important. Others' words were a rushing current, a river swollen and muddied by endless pattering rains. His were a spring that filled slowly. It did not make his words better, only different. There were many things to listen to besides words, but he found that most people didn't even listen to the words, let alone expressions, stance, movement. Others seemed to use the time when they weren't talking only as a space to decide what to say next.

They didn't understand him, but they liked him, and he was content with that. There were many kinds of companionship. He liked the kind he had with other people, and the kind he had with the sky and the wind, and the kind he had with the clay. With others, only the people counted.

Of course, with the clay, it was all listening. People seemed to think he chose the shape, but he only guided it. The clay knew what it wanted to be; he only had to listen. Shani had taught him that when he was very small, when she saw that he could hear the clay the way that she could. Even now, when he first pressed the pads of his fingers into the slick coolness of the clay, he heard the jackal's voice, lively and bright, urging him on.

The bird squawked, and he squawked back and tossed it another grain. The veld was dry, turning the landscape to shades of brittle blond, and it was nice to see a flash of something bright. He had a new pot to glaze today; perhaps he'd paint it with the bird's rainbow of colors.

He scraped the last spoonful from his bowl and was about to put it into his mouth when he noticed a cloud of dust on the horizon. The wind kicked it up sometimes, pulling it in circles as if it were playing, but this was a cloud with a darker shape at its center.

He finished his porridge, set the bowl aside, and waited. As the shape came closer, it resolved into a small figure on two legs and a much larger one on four. In time, the large shape became an antelope bigger than any he'd ever seen, with its head above the person's shoulder. The antelope had a dusty tan coat streaked with a few thin white stripes, and long horns spiraled from its forehead. On its back was a pack made of hide, with a long gourd dangling from one strap.

The small figure was a female leopard, young and slender, with a cloth tied at her hips and another over her breasts. Both garments were dyed red and orange, with the colors mingled in a way that made him think of the glazes he used to decorate his pots. She held a length of braided twine loosely in both hands, and as they came closer, Mtoto saw the twine was tied around the antelope's nose and behind its ears.

The leopard saw him then and stopped. The dust around them slowly settled.

He watched the decision play out on her face. She wanted to turn around, but in the last moment before they'd stopped, he'd noticed something else. Her antelope was limping slightly, favoring one hind leg. She'd probably wanted to rest in the shade of the baobabs, before the animal went entirely lame. Perhaps she wanted to wait a while yet before she killed it for food, to keep the meat fresh. He could think of no other reason why she would travel with it.

He stood slowly. The leopard's eyes and the antelope's held the same caution, as if both of them might bolt.

"Hello," he said lightly, ears up, careful to smile without teeth. "Come sit in the shade and have something to eat. I have plenty to share."

Her gaze flicked to his, then to her animal. "For a moment," she said finally, her voice uncertain, and she clucked her tongue, and the antelope came forward with her. She tied its length of twine to one of the smaller trees, then lifted the pack from its back. The antelope lay down with a snort.

"We only need water," she said. Without the twine to hold anymore, she didn't seem to know what to do with her hands. He gestured for her to sit by the fire, and she did, folding her legs under her in a way that reminded him of the antelope.

He brought out a cup for her and a wide, deep bowl for the animal. She took the bowl from him and held it as the antelope drank. When it had finished, she drank from the same bowl and passed it back to him empty. He filled it again, and she left it in the shade where the antelope was tied.

People loved to ask questions. Mtoto knew that the trick to getting your question answered was to know when to ask. He wanted to know what this animal was and why she treated it like a sister or a child, but this was not the time to ask.

"We only need water," she repeated when he put more porridge in the pot and added nuts and dried fruit. He ignored her and brought out a sack of the grain, pouring it onto a shallow clay plate and handing it to the leopard.

"Will she eat it?" he asked.

"Yes." She placed it in front of the animal, and it chewed the kernels noisily.

"I am Mtoto," he said when she came back to the fire.

"Masozi." She glanced at the antelope. "She is Ngoma."

"You name your food?"

She looked shocked, then angry. "She is not food! Not that way."

"All right." He passed her the bowl of porridge. "There's more if you want it."

"I told you—"

"I know. Eat."

She looked sullen but ate anyway, not stopping until the

bowl was empty.

"You are a long way from the trail," Mtoto said.

"I wasn't on the trail."

He filled the bowl again and passed it back. She glared at him but kept eating. Now that she was sitting so close, he could see that she wore a necklace of the same twine as the antelope's halter, made in the same braided pattern. He could also see how tired she was. He wondered if they had been walking through the night, when it was cooler. That was how he would travel, if he had to go a long way.

When the second bowl was empty, Masozi left the fire and went to Ngoma, murmuring soft words as she stroked the antelope's neck. Slowly she moved her hands along its hide until she reached the swollen hind leg. Ngoma flinched and snorted but didn't pull away.

"I have medicine," Mtoto said.

Masozi said nothing.

"For her sake," Mtoto said. "Please."

She nodded without looking at him. "I'll have to help you. She won't let anyone…"

Mtoto was already running his hands gently along Ngoma's side. Ngoma snorted softly but didn't move.

Masozi knelt beside him. "It started yesterday. I didn't see what happened."

What Mtoto knew of healing was limited to people, but he figured animals were put together mostly the same way. He found the salve Ndiri had always kept on hand, spread it thickly over Ngoma's leg, then bound it up with wet cloth tied with twine.

Finally he passed his hands lightly over Ngoma's sides. He paused, pressed a palm in gently, and glanced at Masozi.

"Yes," she said. "It's almost time. A hand of days left, maybe two."

At last he sat back on his haunches. "You can stay as long

as you need to."

Masozi stroked Ngoma's nose. "We'll leave tomorrow."

Mtoto shook his head but said nothing.

She curled up against Ngoma. Mtoto went to his work, though he came out several times through the heat of the day to check on them and refill the water bowl. Each time, Masozi was asleep in the shade, her hands clenched into fists, like a flowering tree with buds shut tight.

回 ⚙ 回

Ndiri had always said that the people who found their tree were meant to be there, that they were broken somehow and came to be made whole again. Something about this place helped them, she said. Something about being surrounded by the ancient trees, feeling that kind of safety, that sense of time, healed people in a way nothing else could. Ndiri had always been ready for visitors, and though not many came, the few who did were there for something more than food and shelter, even if they didn't know it when they first arrived.

By the time Masozi woke, the sun was high. Mtoto had a fire going, cooking breadfruit cakes.

He put three cakes on a wooden plate and passed them to her. "You should stay until the calf is born. The short rains will come soon, and there'll be more food for her."

Masozi chewed one of the cakes without answering.

Mtoto smiled. "It's all right if you don't like it."

She shrugged. "It's food."

"What have you been eating?"

She stared into the fire. "You wouldn't understand."

Mtoto ate his own cakes, thinking of how Shani had loved fried grasshoppers. There were many things to eat in the veld, and he thought he had tried most of them. He started to tell her that, then decided not to. If she wanted silence, perhaps that was best.

After they finished eating, Mtoto covered the coals and brought out the smooth wooden board he used to work the clay. Masozi retreated to the shade by Ngoma, though from time to time he glanced her way and saw her watching.

It felt strange to shape clay with someone there. His only audience before had been Shani, back when she was teaching him, but even she understood that sometimes the clay would only speak in solitude. He thought about going inside but decided to try and see what happened. He pressed his pads into the coolness and began to shape it, bit by bit, hollowing it out, seeking the form.

Ndiri had always said that sometimes the best thing you could do for someone was listen to them. Sometimes it was the only thing you *could* do. But what were you supposed to do when they wouldn't talk?

He started one shape and then tried another, but this didn't seem to be a day for shaping. He was about to pick up the board and take it inside when he saw Masozi sitting across from him.

"I've never seen it done." Her voice was soft, almost apologetic. "My people weave baskets for most things, even to carry water."

"That takes great skill."

She nodded. "Though there isn't much water to carry anymore. Not in our lands."

"Is that why you're out here alone?"

"I'm not alone. Ngoma is with me."

She spoke as if to the clay, and Mtoto pushed the board toward her. "You can try it, if you want."

She touched the pads of her fingers lightly against it, then broke off a piece and worked it between her hands, idly, as if getting used to the feel of it. "My people tell of a place that stays green all the time, where the grass is never dry." Her voice had the gentle rhythm of a story told to a child. "A place where rain falls out of a clear blue sky, and the soil is rich, and the herd will grow fat on that richness. That is where we are going, Ngoma and I. That is the place we will find, and then we'll return to our people and lead them there."

He had never heard of such a place before, but that didn't mean it wasn't real. There were many places he had never seen, since his travels kept to the same trails and villages he'd followed Ndiri to as a pup. He wondered what it would be like to set out across the veld with nothing more than what you could carry on your back. It sounded lonely, and frightening, and wonderful.

"Ngoma must be strong for such a journey," he said.

"She's better already." Masozi paused. "Thank you for helping her."

"You've had her a long time?"

Masozi rolled the clay between her palms. "Since she was a calf. My father gave her to me, when I came of age."

"A precious gift."

She looked at him oddly, then shifted her gaze back to the clay. "Yes. And now we look after each other." She pressed her piece of clay back into the rest. "And you... You live alone here?"

He nodded. "There were two women who raised me, but they are both gone now. So I stay."

"And you live... in there?" She eyed the baobab.

"Yes. Come and see."

He drew aside the cloth that covered the entrance and led her inside, showing her where he slept, where he worked the clay on rainy days, where he kept his things.

"You have so many things," she said, admiring the clay bowls and cups in their niches.

"I trade with the villages."

"We only have what we can carry." He couldn't tell from

her voice whether she thought this was a better arrangement or not. "We put up shelters for the herd, from the sun and the rain, and sometimes we sleep under those. So strange to be closed in like this, where you can't see the sky." She was almost talking to herself now. "My father used to say…" She shook herself a bit and didn't finish.

"Does your family know you're out here?"

"Yes."

"I can send messages by traders sometimes. If you wanted—"

"No." Her voice cut the air between them, and her ears went back a bit, as if in apology. "They don't expect to hear word of me."

Mtoto nodded. It was hard to think of a family that didn't want to know where each other was, at least most of the time. Once Shani had gone out for clay, gotten distracted, and not come back until long past sunset. Ndiri had paced for a long time and then gone out looking. He'd never seen her so worried, not even when someone was very sick and she was trying to help them. Families worried about each other—but not hers. It was hard to think about, and it was impossible to think of what to say, so he led her back outside.

He spent the rest of the afternoon showing her how his work was done. He showed her the stone kiln outside and the new clay being kept moist inside. He showed her the little pots of glaze and told her what color each one would make. Inside the tree, he showed her the unfinished pots, the ones that had been fired once and were waiting for glaze, and the glazed pots that had been fired again and now were just waiting to be polished and packed into the big sectioned basket, cushioned with dry grass for travel.

"It must be wonderful to make such beautiful things." She brushed her fingertips over one of the finished cups in the basket, then glanced at Mtoto, her eyes asking. He nodded, and she took the cup from the basket and turned it in her hands, running the pad of one finger along the smooth curve of the rim. The glaze was red and orange, almost the shades of the cloth she wore, and something in the shifting color reminded him of the way her eyes flashed.

"It is fire, then, that makes these things," she said, in that soft, wondering tone again, as if she spoke to herself instead of to him.

Mtoto nodded, then realized she wasn't looking at him. "Yes."

"My people use fire, too. We use it to clear the fields. We dance with it. We sing to it." Her voice was so low he strained to hear it. "We know everything it can do. Or I thought we did."

"I can teach you, if you want." It surprised him to say that, but there was such a longing in her voice.

"I won't be here long enough." She held the cup with both hands, as if it held something she must drink, or something hot and she needed the warmth.

"Keep it," Mtoto said.

She put it back in the basket. "I've taken enough. I should see to Ngoma." Without another glance, she headed back to the tree where the eland was tied.

Mtoto picked up the cup. It was warm from her hands. He thought of her drinking from it, thought of it going with her on her long journey, to places he would never see.

Mostly he traded for his work, because there were things he needed. Sometimes it was different. Sometimes a piece had belonged to a certain person from the day it was shaped, only the person didn't know it until they saw it. And when they saw it, when they held it, it sang for them, the way the clay sang to him.

"Like love," Ndiri had said, when Shani explained it to him.

"Well." Shani's nose wrinkled as she thought. "I suppose so. But nicer."

He wrapped loose mats of dry grass around the cup, then wrapped it in hide, tied the bundle with twine, and left it on top of the basket. That pack Ngoma had carried on her back was large enough to tuck a gift in unnoticed. He only hoped Masozi wouldn't leave without telling him.

When he went back outside, carrying a full waterskin, Masozi was still with Ngoma. He paused in the entrance, half-hidden by the curtain, to watch as she tied a length of twine tight around the eland's neck. Masozi's tenderness with Ngoma made him smile; it was such a contrast to the snappish fire he'd seen in her eyes.

Then he saw the glint of the knife in her hand.

The force she put behind the blow looked to be enough to kill Ngoma, but she only nicked the vein in the eland's throat, and a stream of blood arced out. Masozi took up the long gourd from her pack, pulled out a stopper of braided grass, and caught the blood in the gourd. Through it all, Ngoma stood placidly. She had twitched once when the knife bit, as if it were a fly, but beyond that she only flicked her tail and ears while Masozi murmured to her.

Finally Masozi mixed a bit of mud and dung on her fingertips and pressed it into the wound, and the bleeding stopped. She then took what looked like a waterskin from the pack and poured a thick yellowish liquid into the gourd, mixing it with the blood. And then, she lifted the gourd to her mouth and drank.

Mtoto felt as though he were seeing something private, like the time he'd walked up on a pair of lovers in the veld. Still he watched, and as Masozi lowered the gourd, the curtain that covered him fluttered in the breeze. Her gaze followed it, and she saw him, and he saw something in that gaze that was anger and something that was fear. She licked the mixture from her muzzle, and as he came outside, her eyes dared him to speak.

"I came to see her leg," he said. "It should stay wet."

"I can do that."

"I know." He untied the waterskin and poured a thin stream onto the hides around Ngoma's leg. "It doesn't hurt her?"

"Her leg?"

"No," he said.

"I would never hurt her," Masozi said softly. "She is life to me, as I am to her. That is how we live, all of us." She stroked Ngoma's neck. "That is how we have always lived. It does not hurt them. We only take what we need."

"You do not hunt, then?"

"Why should we? The milk and the blood is enough. We trade the meat of old ones, or those who are injured. And we trade the milk, if there is more than we need." Masozi glanced at him, her eyes searching his.

"Others have not understood," he said.

She shrugged. "We keep to ourselves. It doesn't matter. The lions will take ten lives in a night's hunt, if it suits their lust, but they call us demons for living as we do. How can they know? *They* kill everything they see."

He thought of Leya, who had learned from Ndiri and Shani as he had, and how the lioness had always spoken of the hunt. It was in the same tone, with the same sense of sacrifice and even love. He thought of how much Leya and Masozi were alike in that way, and how much they would likely hate each other, the way Masozi spoke of lions.

She had set the gourd on the ground. He picked it up, waving away a curious fly. It was not completely empty.

He glanced at her. She nodded. Everything in her expression, her stance, was a challenge.

He drank. It was thick, and he swallowed several times to

get it down. Salt, and fat, and a faint tang beneath he couldn't place. It was surprisingly bland and surprisingly rich as well. There were worse things, he supposed, to live on.

He handed the gourd back to her and nodded. Her gaze softened then, just a bit, and her stance relaxed. Ngoma might have carried their pack on their journey, but it was clear Masozi had her own burdens.

He shrugged. "Besides, you said nothing of..." He gestured below his waist. He had not bothered to cover himself since her arrival, and she had neither stared nor kept herself from seeing.

She shrugged too. "There was nothing to speak of."

He tried to decide if that was meant as a joke, an insult, or simply a statement. It was hard to tell from her expression. At last he smiled, and she smiled back.

"Sozi," she said, and when he frowned, "That's what I'm called."

He nodded. "Sozi. Will you watch the sunset with me?"

Her eyes that flashed and snapped and glared could also glow like embers. "Yes."

回 ۞ 回

They waited out the days together as Ngoma's lameness ebbed and her calving grew nearer. She watched him work the clay and told him stories about their god of fire, and he sang Ndiri's songs to her. New shapes rose out of the clay. Every day she challenged him—make the shape of the rain, she would say, or the shape of a song, or the shape of fire. He started to tell her it didn't work that way, but then he found that for the first time, somehow, it did.

They watched each sunset together. Neither spoke; it was enough to watch, and to sit beside each other. When the first stars appeared, they walked back to the tree. She still slept outside with Ngoma each night. It was one of the things about her that was closed to him, and perhaps it always would be. It was not her fault she needed to see the sky.

One night, almost too late to be night but too early to be morning, she woke him. "Ngoma," she said, and that was enough.

The moon was full, and he didn't need to light a lamp to see his way to the tree. When he saw Ngoma, saw Sozi's worried eyes, he knew there was trouble.

He had seen many births, but only a few where he was old enough to know what was happening and what needed to be done. "You must keep her quiet," he said. "I will do what I can. Is this her first?"

Sozi nodded, eyes shining. "And mine."

He took her hand, squeezed it, and she squeezed back. Sometimes you needed something to hold on to, just for a moment. "We will do all we can," he said.

He had to hide his own fear for her sake. When you lived alone, you weren't good at those things, but he thought of Ndiri, how she would speak, what she might say, how sure her hands were. Sozi helped when she could, paced when she couldn't, and muttered things under her breath that might have been curses and might have been prayers.

The calf was pulled into the world, whole and strong, when the last stars were fading from the sky. When it stood and suckled, Sozi threw her arms around him and held tight, and he held her, too, though his coat was wet and matted with blood.

Mtoto looked over her shoulder at the dawn. The first notes of a new day's song, and the first moments of a new life. That was a good thing, and he did not have to say it, because he knew she felt it too. Instead he laughed and pointed to the sky. "At last," he said, "you're awake in time for a sunrise."

She threw a bowlful of water at him. He chased her and

caught her and they spun in a dizzy circle, and they laughed until they forgot what they were laughing about, and it was the best sunrise Mtoto could remember.

回 ✿ 回

They named the calf Nyota, for the last star in the sky when it was born. That afternoon, Sozi brought him a cup of fresh milk.

"That is Ngoma's gift, to thank you," she said. "Without you..."

Mtoto nodded and drank. It was sweet, and richer than any milk he'd ever tasted.

She took the empty cup from him, wrapping her hands around it. "I would do something for you, as my gift."

Let them give you what they will, Ndiri had always said. *Even if you do not need it, they need to give it. Do not take that from them.*

"In times of great joy and celebration, we light a sacred fire. And we dance." Her gaze clouded into memory. "None but my people do this, and none but my people have seen it. I would do this dance tonight, for Nyota, for our gods, and for you."

There were no words for this, but he nodded, and he hoped the light in his eyes was enough.

She spent the rest of the day in the veld, returning with a length of wood she then stripped and cut until it suited her. The ends she wrapped in braided twine, and those she smeared with oil. She gathered stones into a small circle, re-arranging them many times until there were no gaps, and then dug the center out to bare earth.

She built the fire in that circle as the sun was setting, and he sat at a distance and watched. First she untied the cloth at her chest and laid it aside, and then she did the same with the one at her hips. A nest of dry grasses was waiting for the spark, and she knelt and struck it into life. From spark to flame to blaze, she tended the fire as carefully and reverently as she looked after Ngoma. Her movements were slow and measured, and Mtoto wondered if the dance had already begun.

At last she stood, stretching into her full height, the light dancing on her spotted coat. She took up the length of wood, holding it in the center, and dipped each end into the fire until it was lit. She held it high, her head tipped back, firelight washing down over her.

There should be music, he felt; there should be drums to mark the rhythm. As she moved into the dance, her body rippling into each turn, the torch moving end over end, she seemed to be dancing to music only she could hear.

He could not look away. He had never seen anyone move with that kind of control, that kind of grace. Her dance shaped the space around her the way he shaped the clay, and the changing patterns of light and shadow sculpted each muscle. Her gaze was rapt, distant, focused somewhere else, somewhere other. And yet, when she tossed the torch into the sky, each time she caught it as neatly as if she had never let go.

When she was done, she placed the torch in the fire, letting it burn. She stepped a few paces back from the fire, chin high, as if bathing in the flickering light.

And then she dropped to her knees, then to the ground, and wept as he had never seen anyone weep before, in soundless spasms that wracked her entire body.

Whatever music there had been was silent now, and he could not imagine what had taken its place. He left her alone, and by the time the fire had died to embers, she had calmed and was staring into it. When he went to her side and offered his hand, she looked for a moment like she didn't know him, but then she let him help her up.

She looked embarrassed, and he spoke before she could.

"You don't have to explain."

Her body relaxed. "I want to," she said softly, "but not here." She glanced back at the circle of ash. "Not now."

She tied the two lengths of cloth in place again and walked with him back to the baobabs. She stopped at Ngoma's tree, speaking quietly to her and to the calf, and Mtoto walked on alone. This time, though, as he drew the curtain aside to enter the tree, she followed.

"May I come in?"

He smiled. "You cannot see the sky."

"It will still be there."

He made a place for her to sleep, but only a few moments after he blew out the lamp, he felt her lying against him. He held her and breathed in the scent of smoke on her fur, and then she spoke into the darkness.

"I don't know if there is a green place. I hope there is, but that's not why we left."

He had never heard her voice like this before. There was grief in it, and trust, and something deeper he couldn't name.

"We use fire to clear the fields. Only the best of us are chosen to light them, to make the path for the fire to follow. My father had always done it, and I joined him for the first time. He was so proud, the others teased him for it."

Such love in her voice, and such sadness. He stroked her the way she stroked Ngoma, settling, soothing without words.

"The wind changed. My father called for us to stop, but I didn't hear him. My fire had already started. I tried to stop it, but I couldn't. Neither could he, though he tried. He tried until he was burned so badly we expected him to die. But he lived. Three others did not. For that, he sent me away."

"Your father?" he whispered.

"Yes. The one I loved most in all the world cursed me and sent me away. I could take only what I needed to live, and because we were already bonded, I could take Ngoma. She is all I have of who I used to be."

Several long moments passed before Mtoto found the right words. "It was an accident. How could he blame you?"

"I think he was ashamed."

He tried to imagine seeing that in Ndiri's eyes. He couldn't, and there was nothing else he could say, so he held her until she fell asleep, and in time he drifted off too.

回 ۞ 回

He was not surprised to see her packing up the next morning. Perhaps she thought she had told him too much.

"You don't have to run away," he said, watching her tie the pack onto Ngoma while Nyota frolicked in a wide circle around her mother.

"I'm not running away. You run away when you're trying to get away from something. I'm running *to* something."

"The green place?" he asked gently.

"Yes." She met his gaze and smiled. "I think we'll find it someday."

It was a joke, but it wasn't. Perhaps that green place was real, and she would find it. Perhaps it was only inside her, and only the journey could take her there. Either way, she would be all right. He was only sorry for himself.

For a moment, he thought of going with her. He imagined all the landscapes they could see together, how the land and the sky would change, and how it would change them. But all he loved and all his work couldn't fit in a pack. Whatever else he might long for, the baobabs were home. He could not leave; she could not stay. That was all there was.

He went back into the tree and found the cup he had

wrapped up days before. He'd meant to hide it in her pack, but now he carried it outside and pressed it into her hands. He didn't know if she would take it, but he needed to give it.

She unwrapped it. The colors in the clay blazed with sunset, the colors of all the sunsets they had shared. She turned the cup, holding it gently, running her finger along the rim. When she looked up at him, he knew she needed to take it as much as he needed to give it.

"The shape of the sky," he said, and held her one last time.

Don't you get lonely out there, all by yourself?

All day he traced the edges of her absence. He wished the wind would sweep away Ngoma and Nyota's hoofprints, and he dreaded the day it would.

Sunset came, and he watched the colors change alone. He had always loved the day's first notes, but now he loved the last ones, too, the ones that lingered into silence, even when their beauty hurt. He had never left his home, had never shouldered a pack, but still the familiar land looked new.

The first stars came out. In the distance, a fire burned, its tiny light like a star fallen to the horizon.

He wished the traveler well and walked back home.

KAMARA AND THE STAR-BEAST

Every third year near the village of Lwazi, the pale golden veld blossomed with tents, some red, some plain, as the *ndiri* and *karanja* gathered. They came together to share knowledge: new ways of healing, new ways of hunting, places where the herds had thinned and where water could still be found in the dry seasons. They came to share songs and stories, to learn news of friends and family.

And of course, they came to eat.

Leya eyed the zebra haunches roasting over the great cook-fire, hoping there would be enough for the night. There were still two pigs to cook, but perhaps someone should go net some fish for stew. That could go much farther than cuts of meat…

"Leya?"

She turned and stared at Bahati as he limped to the cook-fire. "Yaa's whiskers, what happened to you? Was there a stampede and I missed it?"

A chunk of Bahati's mane had been sawed off, the rest of it was full of grass, and his golden coat was wet where it wasn't dusty and dusty where it wasn't wet.

"There was. About this high." He held his hand just above his knee. "Is it time to eat yet?"

"Soon."

"Come tell the cubs a story, then. I've been a wildebeest

and a baboon and an elephant and I'd like to be a lion again, at least for a little while."

Leya passed him a gourd of honey-beer, which he drank in three swallows, and followed him to the clearing where the *ndiri* children were playing.

"Who wants a story?" Bahati asked, and in moments the cubs were gathered in a ragged circle and as quiet as they ever were, especially once a ruddy-colored boy-cub stopped teasing the girl next to him with his pet rock lizard.

Leya settled herself on the ground. There were a dozen shouted suggestions for what story she should tell, but Leya looked to the girl-cub who'd been teased with the lizard, hoping to distract her before tears started. "What story would you like, Makena?"

"Kamara," she said quietly.

"Kamara wouldn't be scared of a rock lizard," the boy-cub muttered, but Leya silenced him with a glance.

"She might have been scared sometimes," Leya pointed out. "Kamara was a great huntress, but she wasn't perfect. Have I told you of the one creature she was never able to catch? Oh, yes. One creature alone…

"This is how it was," Leya began.

◧ ✸ ◧

You know Kamara the Huntress was the greatest of all her kind. There was nothing that ran on land that she could not bring down, no bird she couldn't snare, no fish she couldn't catch. She was strong, and she was swift, and she was clever—and yes, she was proud.

One day Kamara was tracking a herd of zebra across the veld, and she came upon a track she had never seen before. It was a hoofprint, but it was not zebra or kudu or wildebeest or any other animal she knew. And then, as she was studying it, it disappeared, and there was no mark in the earth where it had been.

She found another of the strange tracks nearby, and then another. Always they vanished before she could get a good look at them, but they seemed to make a trail.

Kamara forgot about the zebra she'd been hunting and instead followed the path of this odd creature. It was like no trail she'd ever followed before. It leapt and wound in circles. It climbed trees and crossed rivers. Sometimes the tracks looked like hooves and sometimes like the feet of a bird or a hare or a porcupine, but always she knew it was the same creature by the way its tracks vanished.

For days she followed the trail, eating and sleeping only enough to keep up her strength. She had no idea what kind of creature she would meet up with, and she thought it best to be prepared for anything. She sharpened her spear and her knife and even repaired her best net, just in case.

At last she caught up with it, and if anything could have been stranger than its trail, it was the beast itself. It had the hindquarters of a zebra, the front legs of a heron, the great ears of the hare, the snout of the red pig, and the tough skin of the elephant. It had come to the water-hole to drink, and Kamara crouched in the long grass and waited, watching it. The creature had a white fire in its eyes, like starlight, and so she called it the star-beast, and tried to puzzle out the best way to catch it.

And then, though she had made no sound, the star-beast's ears swiveled toward her, and its head jerked up, and it spoke.

"You cannot catch me, huntress, any more than you can catch the stars."

And it laughed and leapt away—and oh, how fast it was! It seemed sometimes it slowed down or circled back only to taunt her. She chased it to a wide river, and Kamara came close enough to throw her spear at the star-beast, but at the very last instant it shimmered and wriggled and silver scales ran over it in a wave, and it slipped down into the river. Kamara could not even throw her net. She looked for the star-beast, but the water was too muddy to see anything. The star-beast had gotten away.

"I will find you," Kamara said. "Another day."

And so she went back to her zebra and kudu and scrub hare and red pig, and still she slayed each one she chose. But every so often, while she was following other prey, the star-beast's tracks would appear, and Kamara's heart would leap, and she would start the hunt again. She made new spears that were lighter, swifter, sharper. She made others that were heavier and longer. She gathered smooth river stones for a sling and spent long nights awake thinking up new traps to lay for the star-beast. Always it let her get close enough to see it, and then it would bound away, or swim, or sprout broad wings and fly, and Kamara would be left with nothing.

For the first time in her life, Kamara doubted she would ever catch her prey, and with the pride in her heart, that was a terrible thought. At last, when the star-beast had eluded her again, in anger she called to Yaa, and He summoned the star-beast to stand before them.

"It isn't fair," Kamara said. "How can anyone hunt a thing that changes each time, and whose trail disappears? Make it be one thing, and then I will have a fair hunt."

The star-beast laughed and danced around her, moving like silver smoke. "You will never catch me, huntress, any more than you can catch the stars."

"You see?" Kamara said to Yaa.

Now Yaa and Kamara were as a father to his spoiled daughter, and so Yaa said, "I cannot change what the beast is. But I can give him a new home—if that is what you want."

"Fine," said Kamara. "As long as it's far away. I never want to chase this thing again."

Kamara had called it a star-beast, and so Yaa gave it a home in the stars, where it had all the sky to run and leap and fly in.

"It is done," Yaa said, "and it cannot be undone."

Satisfied, Kamara went back to her usual prey. She snared the grouse and the scrub hare, speared the zebra and the wildebeest, netted the wriggling fish, and stole honey from the bees. Still, no matter what prey she hunted, she felt that something was missing. She had long since learned the tricks of the hare and how to keep from getting pricked by the porcupine's quills. The tracks of the zebra stayed the same and stayed in place, and she could have followed them with her eyes closed. She made no new spears, wove no finer nets.

For the first time in her life, Kamara was bored.

She went back to Yaa and told him this and asked for the star-beast's return. But Yaa was as a stern father to his daughter, and he said again, "It cannot be undone."

And the star-beast laughed at them both, but it would never come down to the land again. Some nights, its tracks would appear in the sky, just to tease her, and those are the stars that glitter as they fall, disappearing as soon as you see them.

From that time, Kamara was never as frustrated or angry or tired as she was when she hunted the star-beast. But she was never quite as happy, either.

"And this is how it is," Leya finished. "We all must chase something we may never catch, something we might even think we cannot catch. For if the hunt is in our blood, that, too, is where our happiness lies."

By then the food was ready, and the cubs scattered. As Leya stood, Bahati came up behind her and slipped an arm around her waist, nuzzling her neck. "And what have you chased," he asked, "that you couldn't catch?"

She smiled and touched her nose to his. "Many things, but I think I have all of them at last."

"I'll have to be careful you don't get bored, then."

She chuckled. Bahati went on to the fire-circle. Leya paused, gazing up at the darkening sky. The first stars were coming out, and she thought of all her own hunts, all the stories she had learned and the ones she had lived. For a moment, she thought she saw a faint arc through the sky, like a child's spear, light and quick. She blinked, and it was gone.

WHERE THE RIVERS MEET

Among the packs of painted dogs that roam the veld, it is said that when a girl-child is orphaned young, it is because the gods have called her. She is to have no mother but the sun, no father but the rain. All the gods will speak to her, and she will carry their power as her birthright.

When the swollen river took Ndiri's mother and father, during the time her pack would come to call "the great rains," Ndiri was too young to understand who the gods were, or why they had taken her parents, or what they might want with her.

The duty of teaching her all those things fell, therefore, to her mother's mother, Wema. And so, Wema packed away her grief for her daughter, neatly and swiftly, just as she packed up her herbs and roots and rattles when the pack moved from one camp to the other. She never spoke of Ndiri's mother or father again, and Ndiri was young enough to forget. In time, if someone had asked Ndiri where her parents were, she would have said she had none—though of course no one ever asked. All the pack knew what had happened to Ndiri's parents. All the pack knew that she was being raised by their bone-mother, the voice of the gods, and they knew as well that Ndiri was fated to be greater still than her grandmother.

And so, the pack feared them both.

"What they think of us, what they feel when they see us—

that is none of your concern," Wema told her. "When they are sick, we heal them. When they must speak to the gods, we speak for them. That is all. *Ago?*"

"*Amé,*" Ndiri answered automatically. *I am listening.* But she still didn't understand. She didn't understand why, in both the wet and dry camps, their hut was set apart from everyone else's. She didn't understand why they weren't allowed to touch anything the others ate—not even to dig yams or carry melons, both of which looked like great fun. The one time Ndiri had dug out a yam, she'd had to eat the whole thing at once when Wema caught her, even though she wasn't hungry and her stomach ached until nightfall.

For a long time, she also didn't understand why they couldn't eat meat. The hunters were always bringing it back—zebra, gazelle, red hog, scrub hare—as much as anyone could want. There was plenty to go around, but Ndiri had never tasted a bite, and the closest her grandmother came to the carcass was to touch its mouth with water and murmur a prayer.

Ndiri watched this curiously. "Bibi, what are you doing?"

"Freeing its spirit, so it will leave the body and go back to its own."

"What if you didn't?"

"A restless spirit might make trouble."

Ndiri looked at the gazelle. It was young and would barely give enough meat for stew. How much trouble could it make?

Wema answered her as if she'd asked the question out loud. "It is the small gods that make the most trouble," she said. "Small gods and small people. *Ago?*"

"*Amé.*"

There were gods in everything, Ndiri learned, small and large and in between. She learned to recite their names, both their safe names that anyone could use without fear, and their secret names that only the bone-mothers knew. She learned the symbols that begged their protection, drawing line after line in the packed-earth floor of their hut while Wema waved smoldering grasses into sharp-sweet smoke to keep any troublemaking spirits at bay. There were gods to bring the night, to bring the rain, gods whose songs made the plants grow. The great sun-mother herself had seventeen names, each with its time and purpose. Ndiri recited them until her head ached and her eyes burned from the smoke.

But then—oh, then, at last, when her grandmother was tired or called away to tend to the pack, when Ndiri's lessons and chores were done, she was free. She wanted to play with the other children, but they only stared or ran away from her, so she went into the veld instead, beyond the huts of their camp. Sometimes she pretended to be people in the stories her grandmother told her, the ones she had to recite back until she could remember every word. Out here, though, she changed the words, changed the stories, played them out with sticks and rocks and dry bones. Under the endless blue sky, melodies filled her head, and she made up songs, some with words and some without, and sang them to the lizards and the ants and herself.

She was singing the day he found her.

His name was Ajabu. She knew all the children's names from watching them play. The boys played hunting games and fought, wrestling each other in the dust, pretending to be zebra or kudu. The girls cuddled dolls and made beads and played counting-games. Any of that would have been fine with Ndiri, if they'd let her join in.

Now Ndiri saw him and stopped singing. She'd been singing one of her songs without words, though sometimes she made sounds that were almost words. She was embarrassed, then angry at feeling embarrassed, then curious when he didn't speak right away.

He stared at her. She stared back. He was taller than the

other boys, but besides that, there was nothing special about how he looked. He was bare-chested like she was, wearing the same hide loincloth all the children wore. Still, she had already decided she liked him best of all the boys in the pack, because when he played father with the girls, instead of just dragging home pretend meat like the other boys, he cuddled the dolls too.

"Was that a spell?" he asked.

"What?"

"What you were singing."

Ndiri shook her head. "I don't know any spells."

"Your bibi does."

Ndiri shrugged. "Then she hasn't taught me yet."

"Oh." His ears wilted. He was silent for a moment, and then he took up the toy spear he'd been dragging and held it ready. "I'm not afraid of you, you know."

She shrugged again. "Good."

"The others are."

"I know."

"They're afraid of all kinds of things. But I'm not." Ajabu puffed up his chest and thumped the butt of the spear on the ground. "I'm not afraid of anything."

"Neither am I."

He cocked his head, eyeing her. "Not anything?"

"No."

"Not storms?"

"No." She actually loved them. One of her songs was a lightning song, and she was making a dance to go with it.

"Not snakes?"

Ndiri shook her head. She'd seen one that morning, sleeping in its usual spot under the big rock. She'd wished it good dreams when she passed.

"Not your grandmother?"

"Of course not." Not exactly, anyway. Most of the time

she was just a grandmother, just an old woman stooped over and bald in places where her fur had thinned to the dark skin beneath. You couldn't be afraid of that.

But other times Ndiri saw flashes of something in Wema's eyes, something that could make her look young, or terribly old, or just—different. Other. It happened when Wema was singing as she dried herbs or dug roots, or when she taught Ndiri stories, or sometimes even when Wema was just sitting in silence with her eyes closed. If her grandmother was the voice of the gods, were those their faces?

Of course, she wasn't going to tell Ajabu any of *that*.

Ajabu sat down next to her. For a minute they didn't say anything, and she decided she liked his kind of silence. The other boys were always running around yelling.

"So you don't know any spells?" he asked after a while.

"No." Though all of a sudden she wished she did.

"Not even little spells?"

"Like what?"

It was his turn to shrug. "Like to make me a good hunter when I grow up."

"I don't think there are spells for that anyway." She watched him draw circles in the dirt with the point of his spear. "But I know a story about a hunter."

Ajabu's ears perked. "Was he a good hunter?"

She answered the same way her grandmother always did. "Listen and find out."

It was a story about Davu the Hunter and how he bragged to the gods that he could kill anything, and how the trickster Ekon led him on a chase through the veld, taking the form of one animal first, then another.

Ajabu frowned when the story was done. "But why didn't he know it was Ekon? Every time Ekon laughed it would have sounded the same, no matter what he looked like."

Ndiri shrugged. "That's how the story goes."

"I would have known."

"Because you're not Davu."

The sun was low, and Ndiri followed the trail back to camp. Ajabu walked next to her when the trail was wide but dropped back behind her when it narrowed. They stopped just before they reached the huts.

"Better go on by yourself," Ndiri said.

"I don't care what they think."

"I care what my grandmother thinks. And she wouldn't like it."

"Why?"

Ndiri squinted into the setting sun, as if an explanation would come from it. "She doesn't want boys around. I guess."

"Oh. Well... see you then." He trotted off down the trail.

Ndiri hugged herself, holding onto a sudden lightness. So this was how it felt to have a friend. She hadn't thought it would be so easy.

That night, she fell asleep thinking up a new story about Davu, though every time she pictured him now, she saw Ajabu brandishing his toy spear, chest out and head high.

She was deep into dreaming when her grandmother shook her awake. "Get up. Come with me."

Ndiri dragged herself off her mat. Wema had rubbed white clay into her thin fur, and now she was tying up her hide-bag stained with red ochre, the one that held all her herbs and powders.

Ndiri yawned. "Where are we going?"

"To Thabo's hut. When we get there, keep quiet. Keep out of the way. Don't speak to me, or to anyone. But watch, and listen. *Ago?*"

"*Amé.*" The night was warm, but Ndiri shivered to the base of her tail.

She'd lied to Ajabu earlier. Some things did scare her, and the mask her grandmother unwrapped now was one of them.

It was made of dark wood and hide, horn and bone, with slits for eyes and a gaping mouth. It was mostly canine in shape, though the ears were too small and a double set of horns thrust out from the forehead. Below the face, a cape of dried grasses reached almost to the waist.

Wema settled the mask into place, and then Ndiri knew. This was not her bibi; this was the bone-mother. This was the other and nothing else, and that meant this was no simple healing, no slight sickness or wound to bind.

The bone-mother went to battle death itself.

Amé, Ndiri thought, and followed her into the night.

◧ ⚙ ◨

The hut smelled of sweet smoke and sickness. Ndiri sat on the floor, as far away from Thabo as she could get.

Thabo was one of the hunters. The last time Ndiri had seen him, he'd been carrying back meat for the pack, laughing and joking with the others, reliving the hunt.

She forced herself to look at his leg. The wound was deep, and now it had swollen and festered. Thabo's mother waved sweet grasses against the putrid air, but nothing could cover the smell. His wife and sisters pressed wet cloths against the pads of his hands and feet, but he seemed to take no notice of them or anything else. His eyes were closed, and at times he jerked and moaned, as if dreaming.

The song her grandmother sang—the song the bone-woman sang—seemed to come up out of the earth, a low vibration that Ndiri felt in the pads of her feet, in her breastbone, in her blood. Wema passed a bone rattle over Thabo's body, again and again, lingering over the wound, stamping a counterpoint into the packed earth. Sometimes her song rose to a keening howl, and sometimes it died down to a low throb.

Were the gods listening? Bongani, the protector of hunters? Nomusa, who looked after the weak? Oba, who was life itself?

Ndiri listened. Pulling her knees to her chest, breathing in the close, dank air, she closed her eyes and let the rhythm tug at her chest. The muscles in her legs tightened and relaxed, and she longed to join the dance herself. Was this, then, what Wema felt? As if she were slipping out of herself, rising out of herself?

Time passed. Ndiri's mind followed paths within the rhythm, and then the paths became currents, blending, separating, slowing, surging. She was a white bird soaring over a muddy, sluggish river. She stretched her wings wide, and where she flew, the water slowly cleared, until it raced over rocks and sent up sparkling spray. Again and again, she turned and dipped, circling back along the twisting course. Beyond it, something pulled at her. The source, where the river began.

But her wings weren't strong enough. The force that tugged at her would pull her apart if she got too close, would leave her a scattering of white feathers and hollow bones... She drew away, though she ached to turn from it...

Ndiri struggled to open her eyes. The rattle near her clattered to a stop.

She was standing over Thabo, her arms stretched wide, palms down. She stared at her own hands a moment, wondering why they weren't wings. Then she realized everyone was staring at her.

Wema swept past her and placed a hand to Thabo's nose and pads. She murmured something, and then she spoke clearly, the only words she ever spoke while wearing the mask.

"So speak the gods, in the name of Oba."

Ndiri hugged herself, shivering. Whatever it had been,

it was gone now, and she felt hollow and strange, like something of herself had gone with it.

Wema took her by the wrist and pulled. Ndiri followed her back into the night, all the way to their own hut. Silently Wema removed the mask, wrapping it carefully. Silently she poured water into a bowl and washed the white clay from her fur Silently she carried the bowl into the veld, emptied it, and returned. Only then, when she was Wema gain, did she fix her gaze on Ndiri. Only then did she speak.

"What did you see?"

Ndiri forced a whisper from her dry throat. "Will he live?"

"He will live." There was no doubt in Wema's voice, and that rising feeling tugged at Ndiri's breastbone again. "Tell me what you saw."

Ndiri knelt by the riverbank, letting the slow water swirl into the calabash. When it was full, she set it aside and sat watching the muddy current, thinking about Thabo and about the white bird.

Had a god spoken to her, worked through her? Wema hadn't said so—in fact, she'd done little more than grunt an acknowledgment when Ndiri told her about the vision. Maybe she'd only been dreaming. Maybe the gods had never called her at all.

But if Thabo lived...

She dipped her fingers in the water, feeling the tug of the current, remembering the shiver in her breastbone with Wema's song. She had the sudden feeling of being in a current she couldn't escape, a sudden feeling of wanting to fight against it anyway. She didn't like any of it.

"Hey, witch-girl."

Ajabu's joking voice startled her. She jerked her hand from the water and then, when she saw it was him, flung the droplets at him. "I'm not a witch-girl."

He sat down beside her. "Okay, story-girl, then. Got another one about Davu?"

"Maybe."

"Will you tell me?"

"What will you give me?" She liked this game; it was a tug that went both ways.

"I don't have anything. I'll bring you something tomorrow."

She eyed him.

"I will. Something good." He touched his fingertips to his mouth, then to his chest, over his heart. It was the gesture the hunters made when they promised something, and in the boy's face she saw a glimpse of the man he wanted to be.

"All right," she said.

She told the story, starting out with one she'd learned from Wema, but then adding her own bits, sometimes making things up based just on Ajabu's reactions. He didn't sit quietly the way you were supposed to; he asked questions and gave opinions and something even argued with her, and she argued back. In the regular stories, Davu was something of a proud fool, something like a joke for the gods. She kept him proud but gave him an edge of wisdom, so his challenge of the gods became less foolish pride and more sincere courage. She liked him better that way, and it was clear Ajabu did too. At the end, he laughed and clapped and wanted more, but she stood and picked up the calabash.

"No more today. *I* have chores, and so should you, lazy boy." She liked teasing him, liked being teased, and more than anything liked learning all of it.

He grinned back at her. "Tomorrow?"

"Maybe. Remember your promise."

"I'll remember."

She took the longer path back to their hut, the one that wound through the veld. She felt like singing but didn't, wanting to hold the feelings close and not let them out even in song. Even when she saw the other girls playing their clapping games, laughing with each other when one of them lost the rhythm, for once she didn't mind. Even when they stopped their game and whispered to each other as she passed, it didn't matter. They were only silly girls, after all. Half of them didn't like each other anyway, only pretended, and one good friend was worth a dozen of them.

She felt a sudden picture in her mind—the white bird circling, soaring. She rose with it, half walking, half flying. The calabash of water weighed nothing, and the heat was only the sun-mother, shining grace.

That evening, after they had eaten, Wema called for a story.

"Which one, bibi?"

"Davu and the kudu's horn."

Ndiri's stomach fluttered. That was the same one she'd told Ajabu earlier. In an instant she imagined Wema's proud surprise at her cleverness, and she began as she had before, as the story had always begun. Then she slipped easily into her own creation, watching Wema as she had watched Ajabu, looking for signs of which way the story should go, which parts she should draw out and which she should sweep through.

Her grandmother's gaze hardened. Ndiri faltered, losing her place, but went on.

"Stop."

Ndiri stopped. There was no hesitation when Wema spoke like that. In the silence that followed, Ndiri heard insects thrumming in the veld, along with the rush of blood in her burning ears. It was like seeing lightning and waiting for the thunder.

"What was that?" Wema asked.

"A story."

"No."

"A… new story?"

"There are no new stories," Wema said, each word sharp. "There are only the stories as they are. They do not change. You cannot change the sky or the rock or the shape of the kudu's horns. They are as they are, and if you lie about them, you lie about the gods. *Ago?*"

Ndiri twined her fingers in her lap. "*Amé.*"

"Now. Tell of Davu and the kudu's horn, as they were."

Ndiri spoke the story, though it was like a cracked calabash now with all the water drained out. There was nothing but dust in her mouth. Still, when she reached the end, Wema nodded and looked satisfied.

Ndiri said nothing more for the rest of the evening. That night, as Wema slept, Ndiri slipped out into the veld. The big rock at her favorite spot was still faintly warm from the day, and she sat there, watching the stars, thinking of large gods and small ones, the ones whose eyeshine burned in the stars, the ones in the rains and the rock. If they were alive—and how could they not be—then how could there not be new stories? Otherwise it would be like dreaming the same dream every night. Only dead things didn't change.

It hadn't felt like lying. It had felt like taking a different path through the veld, arriving at the same place.

The rock beneath her had cooled. She shivered and went back to the hut, but it was a long time before she fell asleep.

Ajabu found her at the rock the next morning. "Hey, witch-girl."

When she didn't respond, he dropped his ears contritely and added, "Ndiri."

She realized that was the first time he'd ever called her by name. It was... nice. She moved over to make room, and he sat next to her.

"I brought you something," he said. "Like I promised, remember?"

"I remember," Ndiri said softly.

"Here." He held it out to her, and she took it: a white feather as long as her hand.

She held it loosely, watching it move with her breath. She stroked a finger along it, feeling the taut smoothness of flight. The white bird. The river. The voice of the gods...

"Don't you like it?" His voice sounded both hopeful and hurt.

"I do." She looked at the feather, not at him. "But I can't tell you stories anymore."

"Why not?"

"I just can't."

"Your bibi says?"

"Sort of."

"Oh." They sat in silence a moment. "Well—we can still be friends, right?"

She shrugged. "You have lots of friends."

"None like you."

The bird in her chest leapt into flight. "Really?"

He made that same gesture again, fingertips to his mouth, then to his heart.

She grinned. "Okay."

"Besides, I could tell *you* a story instead."

"You?" She laughed.

"Me. And it'll be just as good as yours."

She gave a snorting bark. "Sure. So tell me."

It was a terrible story, of course, and he got half the names wrong and made the other ones up, and by the time he was done she'd never laughed so hard in her whole life, and when she saw his eyes afterward she understood that that was what he'd had in mind all along.

There was no god for laughter, she realized later. Strange to think of it, when there were gods for almost everything else, when she'd been dry earth and laughter as welcome as rain.

Day passed into day. Thabo the hunter, his leg scarred but sound, went back to the hunt and brought a thin zebra to the hungry pack. The water-holes were shrinking, and it would be time soon to move to the dry camp, to follow the herds as they sought water and grass.

Ndiri walked farther and farther for the day's water, but it was a good time for daydreaming. She dreamed a life to suit herself and reveled in the details. Another pack, of course, and other lands, since most girls went to other packs for their husbands. She would have a sturdy hut, neatly built, and she'd learn to weave the mats to sleep on. She dreamed children, a girl and a boy, one to hold in each arm, perfect babies who only cried when she needed something to comfort. Some of her songs became lullabies. Her husband was left a convenient blur, but he was a good hunter, because they ate meat every day, and they were happy.

In the veld, by herself, she could believe it.

Ajabu was dreaming his own dreams, and when they were alone under the broad sky he told her about them. By the time the rains came, he would be old enough to go with the hunters, to begin to learn how to make weapons, how to track prey and bring it down, all the ways and songs and prayers of the life he longed for. But each boy needed a hunter to teach him, someone not his father or brother, and no one had spoken for Ajabu.

"I want Thabo," Ajabu said one afternoon as they lay side

by side by the river. They'd gone for a swim to cool off and were letting their fur dry before they dressed again. "The other hunters are stronger or faster, but he knows more. And he almost died, but he didn't. That makes him braver, and wiser too."

"So ask him."

Ajabu said nothing, and Ndiri wondered if she'd finally found something he was afraid of. "Are you sure he's the one you want?"

"Yes."

Ndiri mimicked her grandmother's tone. "Then it will be so."

Ajabu's eyes widened. "Can you—really?"

Ndiri touched her fingers to her mouth, then her heart, and smiled.

She knew Ajabu was expecting her to cast a spell, or say a prayer, or do some other ritual to give him what he wanted. Instead, she went that evening to Thabo's hut and waited for him to come out for the night's hunt. She saw him before he saw her, and she caught a flash of fear in his eyes when he recognized her. She still felt strange remembering the night of the healing. It seemed Thabo did too.

"I'm here for my friend," Ndiri said.

Thabo regarded her. That first fear was gone from his eyes now, but he still spoke stiffly, as if he were talking to her grandmother instead. "And who is your friend?"

"Ajabu. He wants to be a hunter, but no one's spoken for him. You could teach him."

"If he's afraid to ask me himself, perhaps he's not ready."

"He's not afraid," Ndiri snapped, and the hunter flinched. "I came to ask for him because your debt is with the gods. And with me."

Thabo's hand went to his thigh, as if the old wound ached.

"He'll be a good hunter," Ndiri added more softly. She

meant it to sound like her opinion, but if he took it as fore-sight, so be it. If they were all going to be afraid of her any-way, she might as well get some good out of it.

At last Thabo nodded. "He may follow my trail, and if he learns well, I will speak his name to Bongani, and he will be one of us."

Ndiri bit back a smile. "Thank you." Then she ducked into the veld, before he could change his mind or ask her anything else.

Ajabu found her by the far river the next morning and took the full calabash from her to carry. His tail whipped up a cloud of dust. "He's spoken for me!"

She smiled. "I know."

"What did you—"

She touched her fingers to his lips and fixed him with a stare worthy of her grandmother.

"Oh," he whispered when she took her hand away. "Okay. But—thank you."

She waved his thanks away, scuffing her feet in the dust as they walked. She felt unsettled, the white bird circling. Was it wrong, to use her gifts—to use the gods—to get what she wanted? Then again, it was only what everyone else did, everyone praying for themselves. And Ajabu had made her happy, and now he was happy, and nothing about that felt wrong.

A few days later, he brought her his first kill, a half-grown porcupine. "I'm supposed to eat it myself," he explained, "but I thought we should share. I mean…" He looked suddenly shy. "If it weren't for you, I wouldn't have gotten this far."

"I didn't do that much." But she took the limp carcass anyway. Something about its eyes fascinated her, how all the light was gone, all clouded and closed off. She forced herself to look away.

Ajabu skinned it clumsily, sticking himself with a quill

in the process, and together they built a small fire, wary of the brittle veld around them. While the meat cooked, Ndiri stared into the flames. Fire had a god with two faces, death and birth. Which one was she seeing now? Death, for the porcupine? Life, in the strength it gave through its meat?

At some point, she would have to tell Ajabu she couldn't eat it. She remembered her grandmother touching the hunters' kills, saying a prayer to free the prey's spirit. Had Wema done that for the porcupine? What if its spirit remained? What if it went inside them when they ate? She didn't know the right prayer yet, but she sent a wordless plea to the gods in general and imagined a porcupine of white smoke rising into the air.

"It's done," Ajabu said, and for a moment she thought he meant its spirit was freed, and then she realized he was only talking about the meat.

He cut off chunks for both of them. The meat was warm in her hand, like false life given by the fire. "Ajabu…"

"What?" He was already cutting off more, chewing on a bone, grease matting the fur of his chin.

She looked back at the meat in her hand. "Nothing." She put the meat in her mouth and chewed, meaning to spit it out when Ajabu wasn't looking, but the savor of it exploded on her tongue, and she swallowed without thinking and wanted more. When Ajabu handed her one of the legs, she ate it to bare bone, then cracked the bone.

"It's good," she said, hearing surprise in her voice.

Ajabu puffed out his chest. "Of course it's good. I killed it, didn't I?"

When nothing was left but the hide and bones, Ajabu took two of the shortest quills for his *jomo*, the bag all hunters carried with talismans to protect them. His first kill, Ajabu explained, became linked to him, and its spirit would help guide him from now on.

181

"Maybe it'll help guide you, too," Ajabu said.

Ndiri figured she had enough guides as it was. She was already feeling vaguely sick, with a cramping pain low in her belly. Was it the meat, or the porcupine's spirit? Would it stick her like quills?

She tried to ignore it and went back home to her chores, pounding yams while Wema wove a basket. When another cramp seized her, she gritted her teeth and told herself it would pass. It did—but then she saw the blood on her thighs. She gasped, and Wema looked up and saw it too.

"Bibi…" Ndiri's heart raced. "What…" She was afraid to finish the question. She'd tested the gods too many times, and now this was her punishment.

Wema took up her bag and her walking-stick and pulled Ndiri to her feet. "Come with me."

Ndiri glanced at the yams. They would spoil, but she supposed that didn't matter now. Shaking, she followed Wema away from their hut, into the veld, a way she'd never gone before. There was no clear trail here, only breaks in the grasses, but Wema seemed to know where she was going.

With every spasm in her belly, Ndiri's fear grew. She waited for the pain to get worse, for it to tear her apart as she knew it must. The gods she'd mocked would not allow her to die quickly. The veld blurred, and she blinked the tears away.

She had no idea where they were, and that scared her, too. She thought she knew every rock and tree to a day's walk from their hut, but none of the ones around her looked familiar. And she certainly would have remembered the rough structure Wema was leading her into now, a hut just big enough for the two of them, with nothing inside but the floor of packed earth.

Wema unrolled a grass mat. "Sit."

Ndiri sat. "How long?" she whispered.

"How long?"

"Before…" She swallowed. She was the granddaughter of the bone-mother, after all. She must be brave. "Before I die."

The laugh rattled its way out of Wema's chest. Something broke in Ndiri, and the tears spilled over. Wema sobered then and did something she had never done before—held Ndiri close.

"It's been too long." Wema's voice was rough and distant. "Too long, and I've forgotten." She cupped Ndiri's face in her gnarled hands. "Hush, child. You're not dying. Not the way you think of it, anyway. I should have told you about it before. I'd forgotten how soon it can come."

Wema had brought a waterskin, and she poured water into a wooden bowl and washed the blood from Ndiri's legs. As she did, she told Ndiri what was happening, how long it would last, what it meant. She showed her how to place the soft grasses, how to bury them when they were soaked through, and that the same must be done with anything her blood stained.

Ndiri couldn't figure out why her grandmother seemed so excited about this. The whole thing just sounded messy, and when she said this, Wema laughed longer than before.

"You are old enough now to see a birth," Wema said. "Rehani is close; I will take you when her time comes. *Then* you will see what is messy."

"Can't we just stop it?" With all the herbs and roots and seeds, there had to be something. It seemed a small task next to healing a putrid wound or breaking a fever.

Wema steeped a dark tea for her, stirred in a dollop of honey, and handed her the clay cup. "This will help the pain, and draw out the blood."

As Ndiri sipped the tea, with its bitter edge lying beneath the thick sweetness, Wema told her more. "You are a woman now," she said, "and this is what a woman must know."

Ndiri's ears burned as Wema went on. She couldn't

imagine wanting to do that with any boy—not even Ajabu. *Especially* not Ajabu. She stared at the tea, not wanting to think about any of it. Her head ached now, as well as her belly.

"I tell you all of that," Wema finished, "because all women must know. That is what your mother would have told you, so I speak for her. But now I tell you what *I* must. A husband, and babies—those are good things for women to have. But not for you. *Ago?*"

"*Amé,*" Ndiri mumbled.

"You are meant for more than that. Any half-wit girl in this pack can take a husband and bear him pups. But you…" She cupped Ndiri's face in her hands again, and her voice dropped to a whisper. "You are called by the gods. That is your path, and no other. You must keep yourself open to them, here"—she touched Ndiri's forehead—"and here." She thumped Ndiri's chest lightly with her palm. "You must keep your mind and your body and your spirit only for them. No one else. And then you will be greatest of us all, someday."

She'd never heard Wema talk this way. Where was her bibi who told her to hurry up, to bring water, to pound yams? She was talking to the bone-mother now—except Wema was there too, in the gentle touch of her hands on Ndiri's cheeks, the new softness in her gaze. Another strange new thing, to add to all the strange new things, the pain and the bitter tea and the pressure of the grasses between her legs. Already it felt like days since she'd sat by the fire with Ajabu, and thanks to the tea, she could no longer taste the meat.

Wema took a covered basket from her bag and placed it next to Ndiri. Next came a bundle of the dried grasses she'd need, as well as a full waterskin.

Ndiri eyed the supplies. "How long are we staying here?"

"I will leave soon. You must stay until the bleeding stops."

"By myself?"

"Of course."

"What do I do?"

"That is for you and the gods to decide. Your voice is strong during this time, and you are open to their words as well. Listen to them, as you have listened to me."

Wema showed her the path to the closest water, and then she headed back through the veld, on that trail only she could see. Ndiri watched her go, aware all at once of how heavily Wema leaned on her walking-stick. Again she had that disorienting, dismaying sense of days—years—having swept by in only moments.

That first night was the longest. The basket held millet-cakes, nuts, and dried fruit, so she had enough to eat, but once she'd eaten her evening meal there was nothing else to do or look at. After sundown, she stayed in the hut, staring at the rough walls, wondering who had built it. Strange to think it had been here all this time and she'd never known, the same way the changes in her body had been waiting. She sang quiet songs to fill the silence until she fell asleep.

The next day, she explored the veld. The closest water source was a stream almost narrow enough to jump across, so small that she was amazed it hadn't already dried up. She imagined Wema telling it, "You must stay for when my granddaughter needs you."

Her sense of smell seemed sharper now, the veld somehow brighter, richer, more alive—though perhaps that was simply because she had so much time to sit and notice things, to move slowly through the grasses. Besides carrying water and burying the soiled bundles of grass, there were no other chores to do.

She made two new songs that day, one with words and one without. The one with words was about Davu the hunter. She couldn't tell new stories, but Wema hadn't said anything about songs. She sang it to the curious porcupine who came to investigate her hut. It stared at her while she sang and then shuffled away, unconcerned. She decided to make a song about it, too, something funny, to make Ajabu laugh.

She wondered what he was doing. Had he made any more kills last night? Was Thabo proud of him?

She knew those probably weren't the kinds of questions Wema wanted her to ask. At different times through the day she tried to sit and clear her mind as Wema had taught her, but then she would hear a bird call she didn't recognize, or catch a flash of movement from a lizard in the brush, and all her attention would be there. Her mind was a restless veld, full of darting and buzzing and snorts and stamps, and she could not quiet it enough to hear anything else. But then, if there were gods in everything, perhaps she was listening to them anyway.

That night, she dreamed of the river.

She was following her little stream, with the white bird gliding above her, and sometimes she was looking up at it, and sometimes she was the bird looking down at herself. The stream was singing to her, a low, burbling, excited song, rushing faster than it ever had before.

Then the stream became a river, and its song roared in her ears. She was not beside the water now; she was in it, and the muddy water churned around her, pulling her off her feet. She looked for the white bird, but all she saw was a faint bright speck circling off into the blue sky.

Then there was no riverbank, no land anymore, nothing but water. She was tumbling in it, nothing below her feet, swallowing choking mouthfuls of mud when she needed air. Something caught her hand, and she grabbed on tight— and the water was gone. She wasn't aware of her body at all, whether she was standing or sitting or floating. All she saw before her was a woman, younger than Wema but with Wema's eyes. She was wearing a necklace of bone and wood, and her eyes were soft and dark as a clouded night.

"Mother," Ndiri gasped.

Then she was on the riverbank, coughing though her coat was dry. She looked up and saw the porcupine watching her. He laughed at her, and she woke.

There were no other dreams, though she almost hoped for them. The one she'd had left her unsettled, and at times— filling the waterskin, or hearing the stream, or watching the sun set—she had the strange sense she was still dreaming. Sometimes, when she went back to the hut, she even had the crawling feeling that the woman—her mother?—would be waiting for her. But the hut was always empty.

At last there was no more blood on the grasses, and when she next went to the stream, she found Wema sitting there, gazing into the shallow water. Ndiri filled the waterskin and then sat down beside her.

"There are two rivers," Wema said without greeting her. "There is the river of this world, of what we can see and smell and touch. The river of our bodies, of the land. And then there is the river of what we cannot see, the river of the other world, where the gods and spirits dwell. That river courses in us and around us, and it is a current we are always in, whether or not we have learned to feel its pull.

"Healers," Wema said, "work where those rivers meet. These times will teach you to stand in both, to draw from both to do the work you were born for. *Ago?*"

"*Amé,*" Ndiri said.

"What you have seen here, you must not speak of. It is yours to see and learn from." Wema planted her walking- stick firmly and pulled herself to her feet.

They went back to the small hut, and Ndiri buried the

grass mat while Wema packed up the rest. Before they left, Ndiri stood for a moment in the empty hut alone, smelling earth and grass and the faint tang of blood that hung in the still air.

"Bibi? Who built this?"

It seemed a long time before her grandmother answered from outside. "Your mother."

Ndiri pressed her palm against the mud wall. Earth and water, and her mother's hands. It felt suddenly more sacred than any god could make it.

"*Amé*," she whispered, and shivered, and blinked back sudden tears, and ran out to join her grandmother in the sun.

回 ⚙ 回

After that, it seemed every day brought a new change. The pack made the three-day journey to the dry camp, where the hunting-grounds still held water. She hardly saw Ajabu anymore, since Thabo kept him busy, teaching him what he needed to know. Ajabu never asked where she'd been those days she was gone. She was glad he didn't, and yet, she'd kind of hoped he would. She felt, bit by bit, that he was becoming a stranger to her, now that he was starting to look more like a hunter—more like a man—and less like the boy she'd known.

But then, she was becoming a stranger to herself, too. Day by day, her body filled out into curves that both pleased and embarrassed her. The girls who'd cuddled dolls now giggled over which boys they liked best from the other packs, and their games had all become silly ones to tell them who their husband would be. When she walked past them, she heard her grandmother's voice. *Not for you. You are meant for more than that.* She ignored the thought that followed, that more might be *more*, but it wasn't the same.

She'd seen birth now—and yes, it was messy, but beautiful in a way that nothing else could be, not even sunsets or the wind in the veld or her own songs. Whenever she saw Rehani nursing her little daughter, something tugged at her, no matter how much she tried to ignore it. Rehani let her hold the baby once, but the rush of muddled feelings scared her so much she didn't dare to ask again.

The boys passed their own initiation and became men. Two of them married almost at once, and giggling girls became gossiping wives. Ndiri stood on the edges and watched it all, feeling sometimes that she stood on a steep riverbank, that to take just one more step back would be to fall and be swept away, as if she had never existed at all.

When she heard his voice one day by the water-hole, she almost didn't recognize it. "Hey, witch-girl."

Her chest fluttered, but she bit back a grin and waited, not looking his way until he spoke again. "Ndiri."

She stretched out in the sparse shade of the thorn-tree and looked up at him as he sat down beside her. "So you are a great hunter now? No time for anything else?"

He waved away a fly that wasn't there, scratching the base of one ear without meeting her gaze. "There's been a lot to learn. And you've been busy, too."

She'd been afraid that silence with him would be awkward, and it pleased her when she found the spaces between their conversation as comfortable as the talk. Still, she caught herself sneaking glances at him—that proud, playful light in his eyes, and the easy way he had with his long limbs as he stretched out beside her in the shade. She caught him glancing at her, too—even staring, once.

"What?" But she laughed as she said it, even as she crossed her arms over her chest.

"Nothing." And they both knew it wasn't true. "Only..." His voice softened, even though he tried to sound light as always. "I feel like we haven't seen each other for years."

"Then you've been walking around with your eyes closed, lazy boy. Bad habit for a hunter."

"Some trails don't need sight to follow."

True enough. She wondered if he knew his scent had changed. It was richer now, more complex, with a hint of pungent musk beneath, the way you might catch the scent of smoke from a distant fire. She knew hers had changed too, to something sweet and full.

Movement from the water-hole caught her eye. A young impala had come to drink. It saw them and froze, waiting, until thirst overcame caution and it walked to the water's edge. Ndiri held her breath, afraid of startling it again. Even at a distance, she could see the movement of its throat as it drank, the twitch of ears and tail against the flies. At last it moved on, fading into the dry gold of the veld.

"The trouble with learning to see," Ajabu said beside her, "is you finally realize how beautiful some things are. And you can't keep that beauty and still have what you need."

She had never heard him sound this way, so soft and sad. She moved closer to lay her head on his chest, feeling his heartbeat, his breath, the river of him both slow and somehow restless. She breathed his scent deep, as if it were a trail to follow, and nuzzled his throat.

He tensed beneath her, then pulled away, rolling onto his side away from her. She heard a soft, strangled sound, like a whine choked off. Then, for what felt like days, only silence.

At last he got to his feet. She sat up, watching. She searched his gaze, but something had closed there.

"I should go," he said quietly, politely, and then he did. She hugged her knees to her chest and watched him move off through the veld. He moved like a hunter, quick and silent, no movement wasted. He had learned so much, and she, it seemed, had learned nothing.

She felt like crying, but no tears came. They didn't even

come days later, many days and yet somehow no time at all, when she saw Ajabu with a girl from another pack, when he tied a necklace of cowrie shells at the white fur of the girl's throat, when the word went through the pack that Ajabu had chosen a wife.

The river closed over her head.

Night after night, she woke gasping, choking on water that wasn't there, nostrils full of mud that wasn't there. The porcupine's laughter rattled in her mind. There was never any sign of the white bird.

She moved from one chore to the next, making each last as long as she could. She worked without thought, because thinking led to feeling, and feeling led only to pain. She was always surprised to find herself hungry, surprised that she still had a body at all and had not become one of the restless, empty spirits of the god-stories.

She woke earlier than usual on the morning of Ajabu's wedding. The last stars were still visible when she went out to the veld. The air smelled like rain, and in spite of herself, she was glad. Rain meant life, meant blessing, and she wanted that for him, as much as she'd thought she hated them both.

She went deep into the veld that day, following one trail to another, humming old songs to herself. Some of the songs felt faded, some felt richer and more vibrant, and others hurt too much to remember. She walked scanning the horizon, as if she were searching for something, and when she didn't find it, she moved on.

She came home fly-bitten and footsore, aching and exhausted. The hut was empty; Wema would be at the ceremony, as bone-mother, to bless the two and open the bride's womb for the night to come. The pack would be feasting soon on whatever Ajabu had killed, usually a zebra or kudu. She hoped he'd killed something bigger than a porcupine this time, or the guests would get a mouthful apiece. She expected to laugh at that thought, but she didn't.

She was sitting in the hut in the dark when Wema came home. Wema put aside her cape and rattles, lit the clay lamp, and by its small flame came to Ndiri. As she had the day that Ndiri first bled, she cupped Ndiri's face in her hands.

"It is done, child."

The words and the touch broke her open, and the tears came at last. Wema held her, murmuring sounds without words, as if she soothed the child Ndiri had been, or the one she would never have.

"It's not fair," Ndiri managed through the sobs, heaving each breath out with as much anger as grief. "It's not—*fair*—you had—a husband. You had—a child—"

"I was called after she was born." Wema stroked Ndiri's back. "I was not called as you were."

"I wish…" But there were too many wishes to speak, too many that crowded into her mind, and again she tasted mud that clogged her breath and water that burned in her chest. Her voice dropped to a whisper. "I knew better. I always knew he couldn't, and I couldn't. And I hate him, and I hate myself. Because I knew."

Wema said nothing, only rocked her gently. Ndiri had the sudden knowledge—the sudden true feeling—that her grandmother had held her this way before, back before she could remember. She felt her mind slip back, just for a moment, to a place where warmth and safety and a full belly were all she needed to feel content, to feel complete. She wished she could stay there.

Finally she pulled away, scrubbing at her face with the back of one hand. "I'm sorry," she whispered, though she couldn't have said what she was apologizing for.

There was sadness in her grandmother's smile. "So am I."

Rains came and passed; rivers filled and emptied. Wema leaned heavier on her walking-stick as the pack moved from camp to camp. They spent as much time in the veld now as they did in either hut, as Wema taught her where to find roots, seeds, and leaves that could ease pain, cleanse wounds, break fever, or bring birth. There were more prayers and songs and stories to learn, and Ndiri soaked up everything. Sometimes she had the feeling that Wema was a cracked calabash pouring itself out, filling Ndiri as quickly as she could so the water wouldn't be lost.

The white bird returned to her dreams, slipping in like it had never been gone. She welcomed it back, that part of herself that touched the world she couldn't see. It reminded her she still had a purpose, still had a path, and in time she found herself willing to follow it for its own sake, not simply as a path chosen for her or as the only one left to her.

Another turn in that path came early one morning in the long rains, when two hunters carried a third out of the veld and into Wema's hut. Ndiri didn't recognize any of them, and when she saw their notched ears she realized they were from a neighboring pack. They must have followed a herd far from their own camp, or they would have gone to their own pack's healer.

The hunters laid their friend on the grass mat. "Snakebite," one of them gasped, still catching his breath.

Ndiri went to the dog's side, checking his eyes, touching his nose. "Did you kill it?"

"No, We never saw it."

Some snakes were harmless, others deadly. But the treatment itself could harm if she gave the wrong one. She glanced around, looking for Wema, but her grandmother had settled herself comfortably in a corner of the hut and was making no move toward anything.

"Bibi—"

"I am not here."

Wema's voice was so solemn and firm that Ndiri stared at her. Wema nodded. "From today," she said, "the choices are yours. Pretend I am not here. Pretend I am a tree, if you like." And she sat back, crossed her thin arms over her belly, and would say nothing more.

Ndiri turned back to the hunter. So far he seemed well enough; his heartbeat was fast, but that could be from fear or pain. The bite, just above his right ankle, was swollen and warm. She tied a cord tightly above it to slow the poison—if there was poison.

When she finally remembered, she felt like either cursing her own stupidity or laughing out loud. Instead, she rushed for Wema's bag and a small hide pouch that held dried berries. She placed two of them on the hunter's tongue. "Chew that. Tell me what it tastes like."

He chewed. "Doesn't taste like anything."

The berries should have been sour, if there were no poison in him. Ndiri nodded briskly; she knew what to do now, even though the hunter was shaking with chills and his pads slick with sweat.

"What does that mean?" the hunter asked. "Is that bad?"

The river of the body, the river of the mind. Some people needed small lies to soothe them; this one would do better, she sensed, with small truth. "There is poison in you, but I will draw it out. Lie still. What's your name?"

"Mosi."

"You must be far from home, Mosi. Where does your pack camp?"

"Near the canyon. We were following a wildebeest we

wounded two days ago. Never found it."

She kept him talking, light and easy, while she heated a cup of water to boiling, counted out five dry leaves from another of Wema's pouches, then crumbled them into the water. From a hide bag tied with a triple knot, she measured out a fine gray powder with a tiny wooden spoon, careful not to spill it or breathe any of it in. From time to time as she worked, she glanced at Wema, but her grandmother was good at being a tree. There was no hint in her gaze or posture whether Ndiri was giving him the correct treatment or about to kill him outright. She had to hope that Wema would say something if she were about to make a terrible mistake.

When she was done, she had a cup half-full with a cloudy greenish liquid. Most remedies she would sweeten with a drizzle of honey, but here it might weaken the effect. She blew across the surface to cool it, then helped Mosi sit up enough to drink.

He swallowed and grimaced. "Bitter."

"Yes. But it stops the poison." When the cup was empty, she laid him back down. "You might feel sleepy. Just close your eyes and rest."

She took the wet leaves that had settled to the bottom of the cup and pressed them into the wound, binding it snugly but careful not to tie too tight. She untied the cord that was already there, letting the blood flow freely again.

The river of the body. The river of the spirit. The body's work was done, and now she rested her palms lightly over the wound and closed her eyes. Mosi was sleeping now, his breathing easy, and she matched her breaths to his. She felt her heartbeat slow, felt herself slip almost into sleep, almost into dreaming. She slipped into the current of the other river, where the white bird dwelled, where she whispered Mosi's name to the gods and prayed for him and for herself.

White wings flashed and snapped, and she jerked back,

awake again. She had no idea how much time had passed, but Mosi still slept and Wema was still a tree in the corner. Mosi's pads and nose were cool, his heart no longer raced, and the swelling in his leg was starting to go down.

She had never felt so tired, but it was a clean feeling somehow, a feeling of completion, of having given and received. She went out to tell the other hunters that Mosi would be all right. Her voice sounded far away, but they seemed to understand what she was saying.

When she came back into the hut, Wema had roused herself and was heating water for broth. Ndiri sat down across from her with a sigh.

"He will be hungry when he wakes," Wema said. "What do we give him?"

"Broth for a day, and snake-leaf tea to cleanse his blood."

Wema nodded and passed Ndiri a small gourd stoppered with a bit of wood. "A swallow of that will bring you back."

Ndiri obediently pulled out the stopper, took a swallow, and almost choked. "Bibi—this is ngongo!"

"Gets your spirit firmly attached to your body again. Very useful medicine." But a smile tugged at the corners of her mouth, and Ndiri grinned back. At any rate, Wema was right; as the warmth of the strong spirits settled into her belly, she felt more like herself again, less scattered, and the edges of the world sharpened up around her.

Ndiri put the stopper back into the gourd and watched Wema stir the broth. "Bibi…"

"Mm?"

"If I'd been about to do something wrong—*really* wrong—would you have told me?"

Wema gazed into the broth and stirred it again. At last she looked up. One eye was cloudy, but the other one sparkled. "I liked being a tree," she said. "I will do it more often."

Ndiri knew her well enough to know that was the only

answer she was going to get.

The pack's next journey to the dry camp was the last one Wema would make. Too weak to walk any farther, she was carried on a litter into the camp, with Ndiri walking silently beside her.

Tension prickled through the pack, as if everyone were scenting smoke but no one could find the fire. These were uneasy, unlucky days, as the bone-mother's body weakened and her power waned. Ndiri went through all the proper motions, drawing the required symbols outside the hut, performing the little rituals to guard against mischievous gods who might see an opportunity in Wema's transition from one world to the next. Those rituals were the last ones Wema taught her, and she learned them quickly and fully and hated every one, more than she'd ever hated lessons as a child.

Old songs came back again. The lullabies she'd sung to imaginary babies now soothed her grandmother and herself. Even the silence after a song was more bearable than the silence before.

One morning close to dawn, Ndiri woke with a start. Wema's hand was on hers, and when Ndiri took it, Wema held her with a grip that was surprisingly strong.

"I will see your parents soon," Wema said. "I will tell them of the woman you have become. They will be just as proud as I am."

"Bibi." Her voice broke on the word.

"I was wrong, you know."

Ndiri forced herself to smile. "Never."

"Oh, yes." Wema's eyes were closed, and her voice was thin and brittle as dry grass. "The stories do change. Everyone's does. Mine did, with you…"

She said nothing else for a long time, drifting in and out of sleep while Ndiri waited, while the white bird within waited, while the pack outside waited. To them, Wema was only the bone-mother, but to Ndiri, that otherness was long since faded. There was only Wema's face now, only her bibi's voice.

"Sing me one of those songs." Wema's voice was a whisper now, a weak flutter of wings. "The one about the river."

It was one without words, and Ndiri was grateful for that. She sang, and she closed her eyes, and she saw a river at sunset, gold and orange, silver and pink, stretching at the end of its course, and beyond it, the sea. The sense of vastness that had overwhelmed her as child now surrounded her in warmth. She held and was held, loved and was loved.

That was the last time Wema was herself, though she lived another day and night. She wandered through the past, whispering broken phrases, talking to Ndiri's mother or to the gods, or groaning in pain Ndiri tried to ease with draughts Wema could no longer swallow. Then she spoke no more, drifting in and out of sleep. The gods had departed, and there was only the woman. And then, even the woman was gone, and only the body remained.

Ndiri tipped her head back and howled a low, rising note until there was no breath left in her. Outside, she heard the pack take up the cal, though their voices sounded distant.

Ndiri rose, her back and legs aching, and unwrapped the bundle of hides that covered the mask. She looked into its empty face. It no longer frightened her as it had when she was a child, but a shudder coursed through her all the same.

She settled the mask in place, tying the strips of hide, straightening the cape of grasses. She looked out through the eye-slits, seeing how they made the world narrow and oddly flat.

She waited to feel something.

She waited to feel anything.

The pack outside had fallen silent. They were waiting for her, for the bone-mother-who-is to announce her presence to the pack and the gods, in place of the bone-mother-who-was. It would give them reassurance that all was as it should be. She only wished she could comfort herself.

She waited to feel the vast waters of the unseen world flowing into her, but they did not come, and at last she knew she would have to go out without them. Her breath sounded loud and harsh, as if it were someone else's. But just as she was alone in the hut, she was alone behind the mask.

She went out, and the pack howled to greet her.

She did not wear the mask again, though she was grateful it had hidden her tears that day. She expected some surprise from the pack at that choice—to say nothing of the gods themselves—but all were quiet. She was grateful for that, too. Already the youngest children ran from her as they had run from Wema. Already they dared each other to run up to her hut, touch the earthen wall, and run back, breathless and laughing at their bravery and their fear.

She felt as if she had leapt a great chasm where her life was supposed to be, leaping from child to crone without ever having been a woman.

The pack moved from camp to camp. Some died; others were born. Ajabu was the father of twin boys now. She was there at the birth and handed the squalling pups to their mother, and turned away so no one there could see her face.

Some masks she still wore.

In time, other packs heard of her skills. She began to travel from one to the next, learning from their healers, teaching what she could. In both learning and teaching there was joy, and in doing her work she felt connected—to Wema, to the healers, to life itself—in ways she could not put into words.

For that, there was still song. She had found a flute among Wema's belongings, and though there was no scent or carving to know whose it had been, the oiled wood showed it had been carefully kept. One night the white bird showed her a young male playing a love song to a girl with soft, dark eyes. She had no way to know if the vision was true, but it felt true, and that was enough. She had never known her father's name, but now she knew his song.

Ndiri let the last notes fade into the wind across the veld. The stone beneath her was still warm, though the sun was dropping into early evening. Crickets sang, and the air and the light were so familiar that she had a shivering feeling she was a child again, that Wema was waiting for her back home, that the young dog trotting out to her now was Ajabu, ready to tease her into another story. Then the wind shifted, and she was herself again, and she saw the notched ear and recognized Mosi of the canyon pack. She had seen him many times now in her travels, though so far he had kept away from any more snakes.

"May I sit with you?"

He left off the title others would have used, and she liked that. More than anything, now, she liked her own name and nothing more, and that was all he used when he spoke to her.

"How is Oyibo?" she asked.

"The tea worked perfectly. She is well now—and as sharp-tongued as ever. Her husband is not sure whether to thank you or curse you."

She laughed. "You must tell him his wife is the salt of your pack. It would taste bland without her."

He laughed too, and his gaze met hers. There was great healing here, too, she thought suddenly. To laugh, to watch a sunset, to sit in silence with a friend.

Mosi sobered after a moment. "We met the thorn-tree

pack this morning."

She knew the answer before she asked, but she asked anyway. "The child?"

"His eyes are still wrong. His scent hasn't changed. They go to their dry camp at dawn, and they will leave him then."

Ndiri had been at the birth, the one that had taken the mother's life. Even now, she could smell the blood when she thought of it too long.

"You did everything you could," Mosi said gently.

"I know."

"For the mother and the child."

She swallowed. "I know."

She looked out at the quieting veld, the sky in shades of fire. It held teeming, humming, buzzing life, great beauty the child would never see. He would never have a name. The gods would take him back like the earth absorbing rain, as if he had never been. It was how it was.

She lifted the flute and played. The song spun out of her, into the wind, into the sky, first slow, then leaping, then dancing. She played the life he would never have, the dreams of a boy and the journey of a man, strength and wisdom and love, for a child who would never hear a mother's song, who would never feel the rain on his face.

She knew the names of all the gods. As her breath failed and the last note choked off, she cursed them all. Mosi held her, and she did not push him away. She did not weep, but her chest ached, and when she met Mosi's gaze, she saw that he wept for them both. They sat that way for a long time, until the moonlight tipped the grasses in silver and the silence between them sweetened.

"Ndiri…"

She knew the question in his eyes, but she let him speak.

"I know what you can't do. But… have you ever…" His gaze dipped into shyness. "Thought of what you could?"

Yes. Oh, yes, and she thought of it now. Her body ached with the thought of it. She could not have a husband, could not have a child, but the veld was wide and the grasses long enough to hide them, and if he were bold enough to take the gods' voice as a lover, could she not be bold enough to accept? The gods had taken so much from her; she could take just one night back. Mosi's scent was strong and sweet, and perhaps with enough of it she could forget the scent of blood.

She was about to answer him, though not with words, when she saw a light coming toward them. It was a torch, its flame whipped by speed.

Ndiri rose and went to meet it. She glanced back once, and Mosi smiled and shrugged. *Another time*, his expression said, but she wasn't sure there would be.

The boy was out of breath when she reached him. It was Tuma, one of Ajabu's sons, and with a trick of the firelight he looked like Ajabu himself, running out of the past to meet her.

"What is it?" she asked.

"Baba," the boy gasped, eyes wide. *Father.*

The wind felt suddenly cold.

She was almost ashamed of herself, later, for running all the way back, moving through the night by scent and moonlight, having left the boy far behind. By the time Ajabu's son reached her hut, she was able to tell him his father had a broken rib, maybe two, but would heal in time. When she told him this, the boy burst into tears and ran to his mother. Ndiri couldn't bear the gratitude in the woman's eyes, and she went quickly back inside.

"Is Tuma all right?" Ajabu asked.

"He's fine. He was just scared." Ajabu had passed out from

the pain as they carried him back, and Tuma had thought his father was dead.

Ndiri steeped a strong tea to ease the pain, then added a splash of ngongo from the gourd to help it along. "What was it?" she asked idly.

"Zebra," he groaned. "I went in too fast. One good kick…"

"Well, you're lucky it didn't kick you in the head."

"I know."

"It might have hurt the zebra." She grinned and brought him the cup.

He had to sit up to drink it, and he managed, cursing his way through all the small gods and half the bigger ones. He took a swallow and grimaced, and his ears went back in embarrassment. "Sorry. I shouldn't—speak so—not here."

She chuckled. "What do you think I said when I burned my thumb yesterday? I think the gods understand pain."

They had to, she thought bitterly, for as much as they caused. If she had lived a normal girl's life, never felt the rivers or seen the white bird, this man would have been her husband. Even if she knew that wasn't certain, she felt it was true.

She took the empty cup from him and wished she could make something to soothe the mind's pain as easy as the body's. She'd thought she was done with this—with him— long ago.

"Ndiri…"

"Don't," she snapped, fearing the sudden softness in his tone. It was the ngongo, of course; she'd seen it loosen men's tongues before.

"I just wanted to tell you I'm sorry. For how things were."

"It wasn't your fault."

"And it wasn't yours, either. I don't know if this will make things better or worse, but I have to say it. You know I loved you."

Loved. Past tense. Of course.

"I didn't want to leave that day. I wanted to figure out some way. I wanted there to be a way for us, but…"

It's all right, she started to say, and slowly, she realized it was. They had both had paths to follow. She had forgiven him, and now she had to forgive herself, for wanting, for hoping, even now. And even now, it didn't mean she had to forget.

Yes, she still loved him. She always would. She could let him go and still love him, and she could love him and still let him go.

He was watching her, and when her gaze met his, he gave her a lopsided smile. "What are you thinking, witch-girl?"

"About a story."

"Mm." He closed his eyes. "A good one?"

"I think so."

"Tell me, then," and in her mind she saw the boy with his chest puffed out and his head held high.

"It is a story of Davu the Hunter, and when he took a wife. There were many he could have chosen, for women swarmed around him like bees, with honey in their voices. They were all beautiful and all clever, and any one of them could have made him a fine wife.

"But one day Davu was out on the hunt, and it was a hot, dry day, and he had followed his prey until the sun was high. He had no water with him, and he longed for shade, and then he saw the tree. It shaded him, and the dew on its leaves slaked his thirst, and its fruit filled his belly. It was a beautiful tree, and Davu decided it would be his wife.

"His pack thought he had gone mad from the sun, but he cared nothing for their protests. He draped its branches with strings of cowrie shells and sang a love song to it. He heard the wind sighing through the leaves, and he told himself it sang back.

"The other hunters took wives among the packs, and in

time they had children, and they were happy. Davu admired his tree-wife and the beauty of its blossoms and the perfume of their scent. The fruit was still sweet, but in time he was hungry for more. He loved the tree, but he was lonely as he sat beneath it. He watched the others with their wives and children, and he knew he had been a fool."

"He always was," Ajabu murmured.

Ndiri smiled. "And then one day he came to his tree and found someone else sitting there first. It was one of the girls he had known when he was a boy, only of course she was a woman now, as beautiful as his tree had ever been, and when she looked at him there was love in her eyes. She told him she had loved him a long time, and she had waited, and she had hoped.

"Davu still loved the tree, but he knew, now, that he needed more than shade and fruit. He took the woman's hands, and when he looked at her there was love in his eyes, too. It was a different love than what he had felt for the tree, but it was just as strong. And the strings of cowrie shells slipped down from the branches and draped across them both, and Davu knew that was a blessing. So they married, and they were happy, and their family grew like the branches of that tree. And every time Davu came to sit beneath the tree, with his wife or without, the tree burst into blossom, no matter the time of year, and each petal fell gently, and sweetness showered down around him."

Ndiri thought Ajabu had fallen asleep, but then he spoke, still with his eyes closed. "I should give you something for that. A gift…"

She thought of the lonely child she had been, the tree waiting to blossom. She smoothed the fur of his forehead. "You already did."

◧ ⚙ ◨

She did not think of the thorn-tree pack's child until two days later, when she was carrying water on the long trail through the veld and heard a thin cry, barely louder than the wind.

"That cannot be," she said out loud, but it was.

The child should have been dead. Heat, thirst, being only a few days old—all of it should have worked to send him swiftly back to the gods. But there he was, though his cries had been without tears and his eyes were distant and flat. By the time she found him nestled in the dry grass, he had no strength left to cry again. He was naked, wearing only a clay pendant etched with a symbol she knew—the mark of Mtoto, the god who watched over children. She wondered who had placed it around his neck. The mother? The pack's bone-mother? She couldn't decide if it was a sign of great love or great foolishness. *Yes, Mtoto, protect this child, whom we have left here in the veld to die.*

She looked at him.

Great love.

Great foolishness.

She picked him up and held him close. His nose and pads were hot and dry. If she put him down, the veld would take him by nightfall, maybe sooner. It was best. Something was wrong in him. He was unlucky, and that was dangerous. He would draw mischievous gods like blood drew flies.

She began to sing, softly, a bit of the song she'd played with Mosi on the veld. The song hummed in her throat.

Put him down, Wema's voice said.

Put him down, said the thorn-tree pack.

The white bird said nothing.

But the woman with dark eyes and a necklace of bone and wood spoke too, and all at once Ndiri wasn't sure if it was her mother or the woman she herself would become.

Take him, she said.

And she did.

回 ⚙ 回

Only gossip travels faster than fire through a camp, and Ndiri was not surprised at her visitor the next night.

Mtoto—as she had named the boy—had recovered quickly. It was considered unlucky to give a child a god's name, but she figured the audacity of it might impress them. Besides, no other name felt right. She wove his name into the songs she sang as she ground seeds of the egusi and mixed them with water and honey, as Wema had done a few times when a mother's milk gave out and no one else in the pack was nursing. Mtoto looked up at her with eyes that looked like he was trying to take in the whole world at once and was dazzled by it. She cherished those first hours with him, as if the two of them were alone in all the world.

The world showed up soon enough, in the form of the pack-mother Lesedi. Ndiri was expecting the pack-father, but perhaps he had sent his wife because this was a woman's matter. The two ruled equally, as had always been among their people.

Ndiri bowed her head as the pack-mother entered. She tried to remember if Lesedi had ever even looked at her directly, let alone spoken to her.

"He cannot stay," Lesedi said.

Ndiri said nothing. What was there to say?

Lesedi spoke more gently. "You know the custom. You know the dangers. Of all of us, you know."

Small gods and small people. Wema had been right once again.

Ndiri stayed silent. Lesedi went on, quiet, reasonable,

cruel.

"You don't have to take him back to the veld. Out of all this"—she gestured to the bundles of drying plants, the pouches and gourds and baskets—"I'm sure you know a way to do it. Something as easy as sleep."

Sleep. Yes. She felt impossibly tired.

"He must be gone by dawn. For his sake, and ours. And yours as well. *Ago?*"

The word startled her, and she answered, as she so often had, without thought. "*Amé.*"

The sky lightened.

Ndiri paused to adjust the straps of her pack and the sling that held Mtoto against her chest. The trail from the camp ended here, blurring into the veld.

The pack would wake soon and find Ndiri's hut empty. She had taken most of her remedies and supplies, leaving some of the simpler, safer ones behind for whoever might succeed her. She had left the mask behind as well. She never wanted to wear one again.

Ajabu would wake soon. She hoped he would find the white feather he'd given her so long ago. She'd left it, weighted by a smooth river-stone, in front of his hut. It was the only way she could say goodbye. She hoped he'd understand.

Wema had been right, as she always was. There were always two rivers. This world and the next. The god-voice and your own. The river of what you chose, and the river of what was given. And the river that seemed to flow away was also flowing toward.

The night before, she had dreamt of new green leaves growing up between white ribs. She had heard Wema's voice again, as she heard it now.

I will be a tree.

And she had seen it, the white bird circling a strange tree, one that looked as if it had been put into the earth upside down. She had no idea where such a thing grew, except that it was not in the land where she stood.

She had no doubt, now, that she would find it.

The sky's edge burned into brightness. Golden light washed over the veld, and a gentle wind sang through the grasses.

"*Amé,*" Ndiri said softly, and their journey began.

A Note From the Author

In creating Leya's world, I've drawn on the landscapes, flora, fauna, and cultures of Africa for inspiration. Some of the names and terms used in these stories are based on actual plants, animals, and terminology from the Africa we know. For example, the Maasai drink the blood of their cattle mixed with milk, as Masozi does in "The Shape of the Sky"; in South Africa an ancient baobab tree is large enough inside to have been turned into a pub; and the call and response of *ago* and *amé* used by Ndiri's grandmother comes from West African storytelling. In some cases, though, words and aspects have been adapted for the purposes of the stories, taken from other indigenous cultures around the world, or invented outright to suit the imaginary cultures of my characters.

Where I have used real terms or names, I have tried to the best of my ability to use them respectfully and mindfully, but I would caution readers not to assume that these stories present a true picture of any of the peoples or cultures of Africa, as that was not my intent. I think of the world of *Huntress* as a fantasy world inspired by Africa, and I encourage readers who have enjoyed visiting Leya's world to learn more about the real people, cultures, animals, and landscapes that make the continent of Africa such a unique, diverse, and beautiful place.

If you've enjoyed this book, I hope you'll also consider heading back to the site where you purchased it and writing a quick review, so other readers will have a better chance of discovering it. And if you'd like to learn more about me, find out about my other books, or just say hi and tell me what you thought of *Huntress*, you can visit my little corner of the

Internet at http://www.reneecarterhall.com. You can sign up for my mailing list there, which will get you a free ebook and keep you up to date on all my new releases, and I'm also on Twitter as @RCarterHall. I'd love to hear from you!

About the Author

Renee Carter Hall was first paid for her writing at age 13, when she and two friends wrote a story that would eventually become an episode of Steven Spielberg's animated series *Tiny Toon Adventures*. Since then, she has continued to write fiction and poetry for adults who never quite grew up. Her work has appeared in numerous print, online, and audio publications, including *Strange Horizons, Daily Science Fiction,* the Anthro Dreams podcast, and the anthologies *Bewere the Night* and *Hero's Best Friend.*

Renee lives in West Virginia with her husband, their cat, and more books than she will probably ever have time to read. She can be found online at http://www.reneecarterhall.com and on Twitter as @RCarterHall.

Sekhmet is a freelance illustrator with a fascination for the natural world. Her artwork is an exploration of the beauty of nature and wildlife by merging fantastical and anthropomorphic elements. She enjoys using illustration as a medium to raise awareness for wildlife preservation and animal welfare. Her work has appeared in many places, such as the "Rare" calendar series, the Anthro Art Anthology, and *Prehistoric Times* magazine. She can be found online at https://www.weasyl.com/~sekhmet/

www.ingramcontent.com/pod-product-compliance
Lightning Source LLC
Chambersburg PA
CBHW070830120626
46556CB00002B/709